HEAVEN

OF

ORUN

(PART I)

KHALED EL HENDAWY

DEDICATION

TO THE SOUL OF MY FATHTER—

THE UNSHAKABLE MOUNTAIN,

WHOSE ROOTS ARE STRONGER THAN
IRON,

AND WHOSE WORDS STILL SPEAK TO ME.

After the Great War ended, everything changed. Continents vanished. Oceans fused. The Panthalassic Ocean rose again. Darkness prevailed.

Like many, I thought it was the end of everything....

But from the darkness—Orun erupted.

Two worlds remained—Orun and Barzakh—surrounded by the vast Panthalassic Ocean, divided by the Panthalassic Wall. In those days, Orun was ruled by King Okasha.

Now, beyond this page, you are about to enter the Heaven of Orun.

The gate is opened....

Step lightly. Some doors never close once crossed....

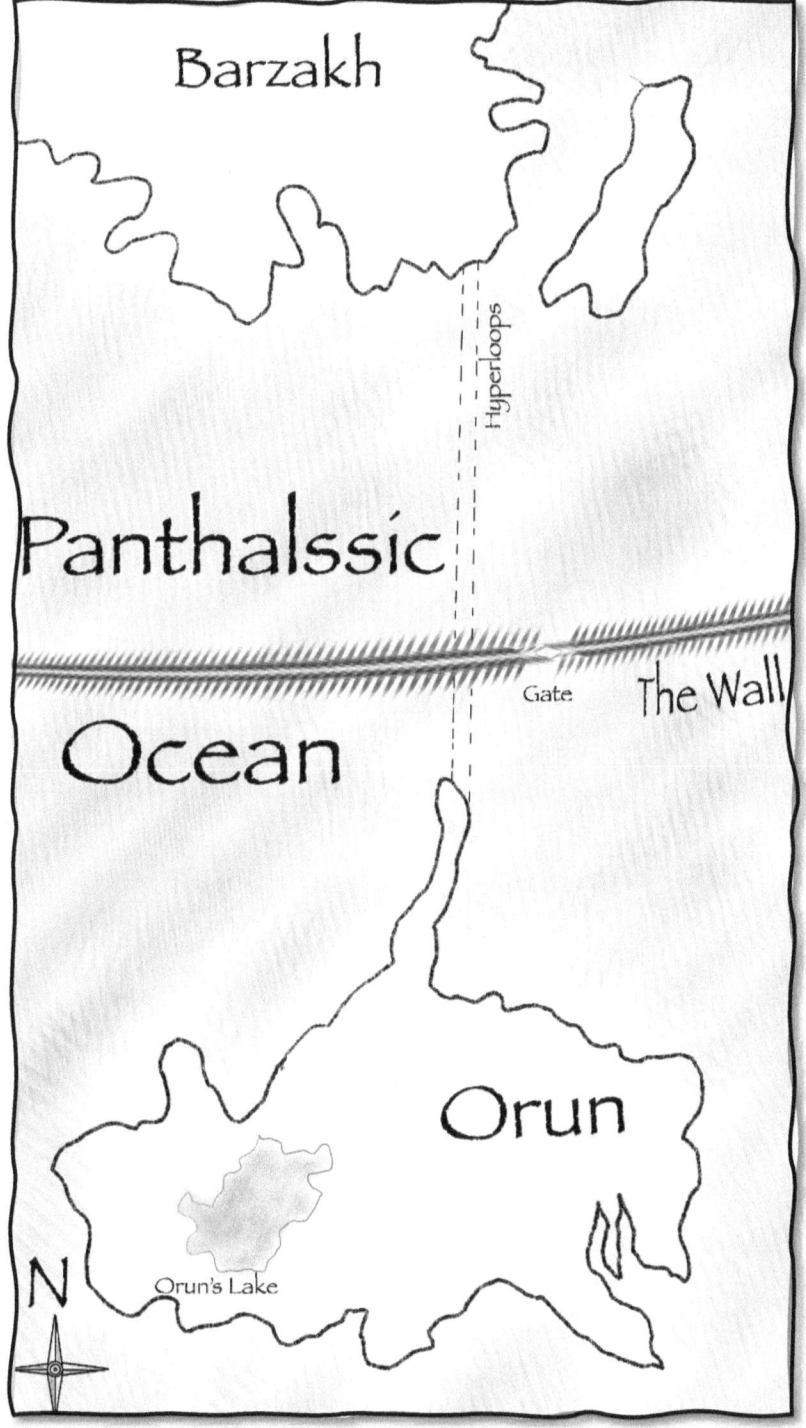

Run Like

a

Beast

Zangbeto

Night Watchers

But Orun… Orun is different. Its story is not a repetition. It is a rupture—an anomaly in human history, unlike anything that came before it.

History is like wet clay, malleable in the hands of those who lived it. But if mishandled, it collapses; and once it dries, it hardens into the past. Any attempt to reshape it then will only cause it to crack and break. And *Professor **Roy Casablanca*** is the *potter* of this story.

I searched for the truth, the part of Orun's history long buried and silenced, until that day came: **Friday, May 5th, 2275**. We sat in a circle around Professor Casablanca. He stood tall, his seafoam beard and silver-streaked hair like a crown, a sage at the center of our gathering. I still remember that day well: the golden light of the twin suns warmed my back, the salty ocean air filled my lungs, and woke me up. It was after a long journey to that place where we finally met. He had chosen this unique historical site to narrate this story. For most of us, the journey across the ocean to reach this place had been exhausting, but I was sure he had done it for a purpose.

All eyes turned to Professor Roy Casablanca. He sat still for a moment; his fingers grazed his seafoam beard.

Then, with a deep breath, he began the story:

Humanity has always built walls: from the Great Wall of China to the Walls of Babylon to Hadrian's Wall. All of them are dust now.

We are now standing atop one of the greatest structures ever built in human history, the Panthalassic wall. Today, it is nothing more than a remnant of its former self, yet it remains the largest structure humanity has ever constructed. And here we are, in the middle of the deep waters of the Panthalassic Ocean. Imagine telling someone from the 22nd century about this wall, they would call us mad.

Professor Casablanca asked,

"But who built the Panthalassic wall?"

One of the attendants replied:

"The Northian people."

He nodded slowly.

"Yes, that's right, geographically, the Panthalassic wall separated the two surviving nations after the Great War." He pointed toward the ocean that stretched behind the wall.

"Above it lies the land of Barzakh, once called Europe. Its survivors settled along the south coast of what remained of that continent." Then he turned and pointed south.

"Below the wall is Orun—*once known as Central Africa."*

"The ancestors of the Northian people—formerly Europeans—built the wall during the Great War for two reasons. First, for defense, especially at the height of the conflict. Second, to stop the Crossers from the South—the last survivors of the lower continent—from entering the North."

9

He paused....

"But when the war ended... the wall betrayed its makers.... Everything changed."

Then he continued,

Before we go further, I must tell you of Unabii, the heartbeat of Orunian culture, the force that shaped its destiny. Some may mistake it for prophecy, but that would be a historical inaccuracy. They are similar, yes, but a prophecy is a divine vision of the future, gifts from the Creator to guide chosen prophets and messengers. But Unabii, according to the Orunians, is something different.

Unabiis are encrypted visions—real dreams that repeat again and again. The same images. The same order. They return night after night, always unchanged, until they disappear. They vanish when the dreamer understands them. ...or when the future they warned about finally arrives, after a great loss, a death, a crisis...That's when the visions fall silent.

In other words, Unabiis are coded messages from the Creator. They come to us in real dreams and reveal important things about our destiny. The person gifted with the talent and wisdom to decode these Unabiis is called a Siddiq *by the Orunians.*

To the Orunians, *Unabiis are like birds circling in the sky, unreachable, elusive. A dreamer may glimpse them, but only a* Siddiq *can take aim and bring one down. This is why they call it "Shooting Down"—the act of understanding the encrypted message behind an Unabii. Once an Unabii is shot down, it stops appearing to its owner.*

*The date is **05.06.2220**, a crucial day in* Orun's *history. The day began with Unabii, but I will not shoot it down so soon. Keep every detail in your memory. Perhaps you will decipher it yourself. Otherwise, I will reveal its codes at the end of this story.*

Unabii#

The owner of this Unabii saw himself tilting his head back, gazing into the sky. It was a deep blue, not dark, but endless. The sky above was not the sky he knew. There were no clouds, no sun, no moon, nothing but an infinite blue expanse. A strange feeling crept over him; his body felt foreign, and his own skin was unfamiliar. He raised both hands, examining them carefully. His feeling was right. This was not his skin. The color was different, yet the palmar creases remained the same.

Suddenly, he lost his balance. His stomach lurched as he looked down; he was standing on a globe. Earth. It tilted and swung beneath him, making it nearly impossible to keep his footing. The gravitational pull was overwhelming, the motion relentless. His heart pounded in his throat, he breathed like a dog, and his body steamed. He wanted it to end. He wished for the Earth to swallow him whole, to put an end to this torment. Then, as if answering his silent plea, the globe steadied, and the violent motion ceased.

But before he could feel relief, something cold and tight gripped his wrists. He raised his hands to see rusty cuffs and thick chains binding him. And then, without warning, he was lifted into the sky. The pull was strong. He squinted, trying to see what was hauling him upward, but his vision was hazy, distorted. He could barely breathe. As he ascended, the air grew thinner and colder. His chest felt heavy, as if a great stone had been placed upon it. And then, from every opening in his body, his ears, nose, and mouth, saltwater began to pour.

But now his vision finally cleared.

Hovering above him, its enormous wings outstretched, was a bird the size of a whale, dragging him higher and higher into the sky. They approached the edges of Earth's atmosphere, the world shrinking below them.

Then, the bird slowed, not to stop, but to avoid something. An upside-down mountain loomed ahead, its base anchored to the sky itself. The bird veered, maneuvering around it, and then, without warning, it let him go.

He was pulled into the mountain, into its cave, and then, he fell.

Exhausted from the ascent, his body felt too heavy to resist. His eyes barely stayed open. He wasn't sure if he could survive the fall.

Then—impact.

But it came too soon, far too soon. And yet, the collision was smooth and painless.

He was still alive.

Turning his body, he tried to see where he had landed. He was suspended in the middle of the sky, but beneath him was not Earth.

He had landed on a cloud. But he was helpless. He couldn't move, couldn't stand. He had to descend, somehow.

Then, out of nowhere, a hand grasped his clothes and pulled him upright. #

The owner of this Unabii was Nuro, son of Okasha, King of Orun's Heaven. But when he saw his Unabii for the first time, he was trapped alone, in a dark place. The darkness was absolute. No light, no space, no sound, just an overwhelming sense of being held prisoner in a place that was both a part of him and separate from him.

He could barely move. His body was folded into itself, limbs pressed tight against his chest. The walls of this place pushed inward, little by little, making the small space even smaller.

The pressing increased.

It pressed against his ribs, squeezed his legs against his body, wrapped around him like an invisible force determined to crush him. He tried to breathe, but his chest couldn't expand.

He tried to cry out, but there was no air, no voice, no sound. His lungs burned, his heartbeat slowed, and his skin turned cold. He wanted to fight, but his body was no longer his own, just a fragile thing, suffocating inside an unseen force.

Then, just as his consciousness slipped, the walls of that place collapsed inward.

He was pushed out.

A sudden pressure burst shoved him from the pressing darkness into something colder, brighter, and larger. Air. He was free, but something still held him back, something wrapped around his neck, pulling him toward the void he had just escaped.

It was the umbilical cord. It tightened around his throat, refusing to let go. It was thick, stiff, unnatural, coiling around him like a serpent. He was dying. Amara felt it before she saw him, the unnatural coldness of his skin.

Then—she saw him.

Her baby. Silent. Blue. Lifeless.

A cry caught in her throat, her body shaking, but before she could scream, Okasha gripped her hands, his own breathing unsteady. *"Stay calm,"* he whispered, but his words meant nothing.

The midwives did not hesitate. One of them reached for the cord, desperate to loosen it, but it would not yield. It was hardened and knotted, something that did not want to let go.

They had no choice.

A blade flashed, then the cord was detached.

But the silence remained. Nuro's chest didn't rise. He didn't gasp. Didn't move.

Two hands wrapped around Nuro's tiny body, pressing desperately against his chest. Compressions. A breath. Compressions. A breath. Again. Again. Again.

His parents' hearts were in their feet.

Okasha's voice came, low, unsteady: *"Should I call the healer?"*

"We already have," one of the midwives answered, her hands never stopping.

Seconds felt like eternity. Then, the healer arrived. Without hesitation, he joined the midwives, his hands pressing over Nuro's tiny chest, reinforcing the rhythm. Compressions. A breath. Compressions. A breath. Again. Again. Again.

Then, a knock.

No one reacted.

Then, a second knock. Louder. Urgent. But no one turned their head.

Until finally, the healer spoke without looking up.

"Open the door."

Okasha moved as if in a trance, walking toward the door while Amara never took her eyes off Nuro's motionless form. The door creaked open.

A soldier stepped inside, his face pale, voice hushed. *"My Majesty, I am truly sorry. This is not the right moment, but we are under attack."*

Okasha froze. His pupils dilated, his mind suddenly split between the battle outside and the battle inside this room. Then, Amara's voice cut through the tension, soft but resolute.

"You should go."

Okasha turned. She was still gripping Nuro's tiny hand, her own trembling. He hesitated.

She squeezed his fingers. ***"Go."*** And he left.

Outside the room, Okasha's sons; Chad and Fahd waited. Okasha was gone, but his heart and mind remained with Amara and Nuro. Chad, the eldest of his brothers, followed his father and the soldier, his steps quick, almost desperate to keep up. He had no idea what had happened yet, only that something was wrong.

The soldier said nothing. He walked ahead in silence, his posture straight, waiting for Okasha to ask first. But Okasha did not ask. Instead, the soldier broke the silence. *"My Majesty, I suggest we do a field tour of the attacked site with the Dragon."*

Okasha nodded. *"For sure."*

Chad's heart raced. For as long as he could remember, he had dreamed of riding a Dragon. He had seen them before, watching from the rooftops as they soared through the sky, their sleek bodies cutting through the wind like living creatures. But he had never been inside one. As they approached the Dragon's entrance, Chad stepped forward instinctively, eager to follow them inside.

The soldier stopped him with a firm hand. *"It could be dangerous there,"* he said. Chad's face tensed in frustration, but before he could protest, Okasha's voice cut through the air. *"He is twelve. Let him in."*

Chad didn't wait for a second invitation. He just jumped into the Dragon. The interior was not what he expected. It was narrow, translucent, and humming with unseen energy.

The pilot received clearance. The Dragon lifted smoothly into the air, as if floating rather than flying. Chad sat by the window. A soldier sitting across from him smirked at his excitement.

"First time in a Dragon?" the soldier asked.

Chad barely nodded, his eyes locked on the world outside.

The soldier chuckled. *"Let me explain how it floats in the air."*

Chad wasn't listening. The soldier continued anyway. *"This aircraft is made from Gravitron, the anti-gravity element. Without weapons and passengers, its actual weight is only one and a half pounds, lighter than a helium balloon."* Chad heard the words but didn't care. The land below was shrinking, stretching into a vast, endless horizon. The soldier paused mid-explanation, noticing Chad's lack of interest.

He smiled to himself and leaned back. Some things didn't need to be explained. Chad was living his dream.

Okasha stood inside the Dragon, staring at the soldier delivering the report.

"WAOFO is responsible for the attacks," the pilot said. *"They hit the gates of Panthalassic wall and the Hyperloops beneath the water. Now we have a breach in the wall."*

Okasha's jaw tightened, his mind already calculating the next step. Then, the pilot hesitated before adding, *"We also have crossers on a boat past the wall."* For a moment, Okasha said nothing. His gaze shifted toward the window.

"Go to them first," he finally ordered. The Dragon adjusted its course.

Not far from the southern side of the Panthalassic wall, a single overcrowded boat drifted aimlessly. It had crossed the wall, carrying over 500 desperate souls, though it was built for only 150. The deck was so packed that people could not sit. Mothers clutched their children, some too weak to cry anymore. Others stood, their bodies brushing against one another with every sway of the waves. They had been adrift for three days, the deep ocean their only companion.

The heat of the twin suns burned their skin, their lips cracked from dehydration. Every last drop of spared water had been given to the children; the adults had none left. The boat was silent, save for the soft whimpers of the weakest children. Their mothers held them close, whispering prayers between parched lips.

Then, something floated up from the ocean. A small, sealed parcel broke the surface, bobbing in the waves a few feet from the boat. Then, another. And another. Within seconds, hundreds of parcels surfaced, drifting all around them. For a moment, no one moved.

Then, chaos broke out.

Men threw themselves into the water, splashing wildly toward the floating boxes. Their arms cut through the waves, clawing to grab hold and bring anything back to the boat. A man heaved himself over the deck and ripped open a parcel with shaking hands. Others gathered around, breathless, waiting.

Inside, lyophilized eggs. Just powder. For a moment, they hesitated. Then, hunger won. They shoved the powder into their mouths, not caring that—without water— it clung to their tongues and clogged their throats. It could have choked them. It almost did. But still, they kept swallowing. Their hands and faces were coated with powder. Another parcel was torn open— more powder. A third, dehydrated food.

No water. No relief.

One by one, the parcels were thrown back into the ocean, splashing uselessly as cries of frustration turned into sobs. The children wailed louder, and the mothers were helpless. They had no choice but to pray harder. Hands rose into the sky.

"Oh Creator... our Creator... help us. Save us. We left our diseased land... spare our children..." Their voices rose together, desperate, aching.

Then, a vibration in the air. It started low, almost like a distant storm rumbling over the horizon. The wind shifted. The water stirred. The vibration grew louder. Someone looked up. Then they saw it.

A Dragon.

The noise grew deafening as the Dragon approached, its massive body casting a shadow over the helpless boat. Some crossers froze in terror. Others screamed. Then, one man jumped into the water. Then another. Fear spread like wildfire, people throwing themselves overboard, swimming to get away. They knew what came next. The Dragon lowered its altitude, angling downward.

It's an attack position.

On the boat, the mothers clutched their children. There was nowhere to run, so they closed their eyes. Above them, the Dragon hovered still for a moment, then released something.

The crossers who had jumped into the water watched in horror, their breath caught in their throats. One of them turned his head away, unable to bear the explosion.

A bomb.

Another screamed, "NO! NO!"

Then, silence.

The explosion never came. Those who jumped into the water turned back. Their eyes widened. The mothers on the boat were dancing. They were pointing at the jumpers, shouting for them to return. Some of the jumpers hesitated, stayed in the water, unsure if they were hallucinating. Then, they saw the truth. The bomb wasn't a bomb. It was a package. And then, another package fell. Then another.

Inside the Dragon, Okasha gave the order.

"Drop more water and life jackets." The soldier obeyed, sending salvation raining from the sky.

The mothers wept, but this time, it was not from fear.

The pilot turned to Okasha. *"The parcels came from the exploded Hyperloop under the water,"* he explained. Okasha nodded, his mind still processing the scale of destruction. *"Fly to the Panthalassic wall,"* he ordered. *"And send more Dragons for the crossers."*

The Dragon adjusted course, lifting higher before tilting northward. Chad watched from his window, his fingers gripping the armrests of his seat.

They descended slowly; the Dragon came to a stop—on the water. The soldier seated across from Chad met his gaze, noticing how his hands clenched the chair's arms, knuckles turning pale.

He smirked. *"We won't sink,"* he said. *"The Dragon can stand on water."* Chad didn't react at first, still unsure.

"Thanks to Gravitron," the soldier continued, *"It keeps us balanced."* The explanation was cut short when the soldier noticed something; this time, Chad was actually listening. He had been disinterested before, but now, for the first time, he leaned forward slightly, absorbing the information.

The pilot's voice interrupted the moment. *"My Majesty, we don't have a clear view of the damage from here."*

Okasha sighed, then motioned forward. *"Lift us again."*

The Dragon ascended smoothly, tilting toward the towering Panthalassic wall.

"Seatbelts," the pilot instructed. The soldier checked Chad's belt, then Okasha's, before securing his own.

As they got closer to the damaged part at the gate of the Panthalassic wall, the Dragon turned vertical. It lined up with the wall's surface. For a moment, Chad's breath caught. His back slammed into the seat, tense and stiff. The pressure felt unnatural, as if gravity had turned on him. The whole world tilted, and his body reeled, unable to understand why everything suddenly felt upside down. The soldier noticed.

"The Dragon can stick to walls too," The soldier said, his voice calm, almost amused. *"We won't fall."*

Slowly, Chad exhaled. His fear began to fade as realization set in.

Okasha didn't linger. He observed the damage for a brief moment before turning to the pilot. *"Arrange a meeting with the Barzakh leaders,"* he instructed. *"And take us back."*

Across the vast lands of Orun, within the sacred hall of the Tribe's Home, the leaders of the eight ruling tribes gathered. The *Dinka,* Amázigh, *Nubian, Berbers, Maasai, Zulu, Yoruba, and Somali* leaders sat in their designated places, waiting.

The air was restless. The Tribe's Home was a place of tradition, respect, and silence. But tonight, it wasn't. Rumors slithered like a sickness through the kingdom, whispered from one anxious mouth to the next.

Some whispered that Nuro was dead, buried in secret, without a grave or a farewell. Others murmured in hushed voices that the crossers had attacked the Dragon and that Okasha had fallen into the ocean. The tribal leaders exchanged glances, their expressions torn between unease and disbelief.

Okasha had promised to address the kingdom at first sunset. People gathered. Waited. The first sun had already sunk completely, and the second sun—the twin—was on its way down. Still, he had not arrived. Still, no message, no apology.

The whispers grew louder, the uncertainty thicker.

By the time the twin suns had set, all eyes turned toward the entrance. Chad entered.

For a brief moment, the hall stood frozen. Then, Okasha appeared. He did not come alone. He carried a baby cast of papyrus.

Inside—Nuro. He was alive. His tiny figure lay cradled within the woven frame, wrapped in soft cloth. The rumors were destroyed in an instant.

Okasha stepped forward, his voice steady:

"We are the Orunians. *The sons of Africans. The first human civilization to walk this Earth. We are the last surviving human civilization. While others burned their lands, we nurtured ours. While others waged endless wars, we built peace.*

"But today, the evil face of WAOFO revealed itself."

"How much hatred must a people hold to strike at unity? At peace? They destroyed their own lands, and now they seek to poison ours."

"But they forget one truth—He who spreads poison... must taste it first."

Okasha raised his hand, commanding the room.

"Today, we make decisions that will shape the future of Orun."

The hall stood still.

Then, with firm resolve, he declared:

"WAOFO are shadowists. All their activities and symbols are banned."

"The Panthalassic wall will close, temporarily."

"And our food supply to Barzakh will not stop, it will increase."

A sharp pause. Then, he raised his right fist high.

"Orun *Daima!*"

A unified roar followed.

"Orun *Daima!* Orun *Daima!*"

The eight tribal leaders struck the ground with their wooden staffs, signaling their approval. Then, the entire hall erupted.

"*Daima! Daima! Daima!*"

Their voices thundered through the walls, shaking the very foundation of the Tribe's Home.

Orun had spoken.

Monday, September 19, 2240. Twenty years had passed since the last WAOFO attacks. Today is *Homowo* Day. For those who did not know this celebration, it was one of the oldest in human history, a tradition passed down for thousands of years, reborn after the Great War. For the Orunians, it was more than just a festival. It marked the end of famine, a victory of survival. This ritual came from their ancient Ga ancestors, who celebrated their escape from starvation long ago.

Thousands had gathered along the shores of Orun's sacred lake. Drums pounded through the earth, voices rose in rhythm, and feet moved in unison, creating a wave of dancing bodies stretching as far as the eye could see.

Zangbeto—the guardians of the night—moved among the people. Their presence felt sacred and mysterious. Those tall straw structures whirled, spun, and twisted. They were faceless, ageless, and timeless. The children, however, were more curious than afraid about *Zangbeto*. They did not watch the dance. Instead, they lay flat on the ground, squinting, peering beneath the spinning Zangbeto, searching for the legs of the one who moved it.

Then, a horn sounded. The Zangbeto froze in place.

Laughter erupted. The children rushed in, pushing and shoving. They wanted to knock down the **Zangbeto** structure to reveal the dancer inside.

But when it finally tipped over, there was nothing. Empty. No dancer inside.

Silence.

Then, shrieks of delight.

They jumped, clapped, and cheered, running in circles as the Zangbeto was lifted back upright, ready to dance again.

At the far end of Orun's lake, beneath an elaborately carved ebony canopy, the ruling class stood in waiting. Okasha stood at the center, his sons Fahd and Chad by his side, Amara to his left, and the eight tribal leaders standing in a straight line before them. The men wore their finest traditional Orunian clothing, **Isiagu** tunics embroidered with golden patterns.

But today, all eyes were on Chad.

He had prepared meticulously for this moment, cutting his hair shorter, shaping his goatee to match the man standing beside him. Okasha's son—his perfect mirror. A Stingray-Rider, just like his father.

On the opposite side of the lake, another group stood waiting, but not for a speech. They waited for the race.

Nuro stood among them, bare-chested, muscles tense.

Beside him, Kato, his younger brother, lay sprawled on the ground like a seal during mating season, arms folded behind his head, completely unbothered.

The competitors were not about to swim across the lake. They were about to skim.

Gravitron. The anti-gravity element. The key to crossing the lake without sinking. The key to winning.

But Nuro wasn't thinking about the race. Because he saw her, on his right, standing just a few feet away, was a girl with buffalo eyes. The world around her faded for a moment, dissolving into the background of noise, sun, and water.

He could only see half of her face, sharp yet soft. He stared, mesmerized, forgetting everything else. He waited, waited for her to turn fully so that he could see all of her. But before she did, Kato's voice shattered the moment.

"Nuro! Nurooo! Nuroooo!"

No response.

"Nuro, *damn it! Hallo?!*"

Nuro blinked, his gaze breaking away from the girl. Slowly, he turned to Kato.

"What do you want, man?" Nuro asked, his voice slightly irritated.

Kato smirked. *"Ahh... Are you prepared,* Nuro*?"*

Nuro sighed. *"Kato. That's the tenth time you've asked me if I'm prepared. I think that's enough now, right?"*

For a moment, silence stretched between them. Then, a mischievous idea crept into Nuro's mind. He glanced at his brother, considering it.

"If I give him an extra dose of Gravitron spray—like the one I use for my horse—he'll be too focused on walking across the lake. Then, he'll finally stop bothering me with all his endless questions…"

Nuro smirked. He reached into his side bag, pulling out the spray.

"Kato! Get up, man! I think you need an extra dose of Gravitron." Nuro grinned, holding up the small vial. *"I've got some to spare. Take this, just all of it. With this extra boost, you'll be running across the lake like a damn horse. Not a single problem."*

Kato hesitated for a second, narrowing his eyes. Then, his curiosity won over. He grabbed the spray with an eager nod, shaking it before spraying it over his feet.

Nuro grinned wider, folding his arms.

"Katooo… Spray your whole body, man." He smirked. *"You know you're overweight."*

Kato froze mid-spray, scowling. Then, he sprayed himself from head to toe.

As Nuro handed him the vial, the girl with buffalo eyes flicked her gaze toward them. For a fleeting second, her eyes lingered.

A brief flicker of surprise crossed her face. Then, just as quickly, it was gone. She turned away, refocusing ahead.

The horn blasted. A roar of movement followed, as hundreds of competitors surged forward, kicking off the ground and launching themselves onto the water.

The order collapsed.

The first wave of competitors barely lasted seconds. Dozens instantly lost their balance, their feet failing to stabilize the water surface. One by one, they plunged beneath the water, their bodies vanishing instantly eliminated.

Only a few advanced, their movements cautious, each step placed as though walking a tightrope suspended over an abyss.

Back on the shoreline, Kato hesitated. He had waited too long. The moment he stepped onto the water, his foot slipped. His legs shot forward, skimming across the slick surface like a stone skipping across a lake. With a yelp, his entire body followed, crashing flat onto the water's surface with a loud thud.

But unlike the others, he didn't sink.

The Gravitron overdose Nuro had given him kept him afloat, but not in the way he had hoped.

Kato didn't run across the water like a champion. Instead, he floated awkwardly on his belly. His body glided uncontrollably, like an overturned boat caught in a current.

Panic set in. He flailed his arms helplessly, trying to gain control, but the more he moved, the more he slid forward, unable to stand or stop himself.

From behind, Nuro burst into laughter. He had expected some clumsiness, but this, this was beyond imagination.

Without hesitation, Nuro stepped forward and gave Kato a swift kick. The force sent Kato skimming even faster, his body racing forward like a human raft, entirely at the mercy of the lake, toward the finish line.

Nuro stepped forward carefully, feeling the lake's surface shift beneath him. Every movement had to be calculated, and every step had to be placed with perfect balance.

Then, something caught his attention. A few feet ahead, a competitor was approaching the buffalo-eyed girl. She stood perfectly still, just as the man neared her, she pointed toward his feet and said,

"Watch your step."

The man instinctively glanced down, confused. It was too late. His balance snapped, his footing wavered, and in a second, he was slipping, plunging into the water with a loud splash.

Nuro narrowed his eyes, intrigued. Moments later, another competitor approached her.

She turned her head slightly and, in the same calm tone, repeated:

"Watch your step."

Like clockwork, the competitor's gaze dropped. And just like before, he lost balance, faltered, and fell.

Nuro smirked. So that's her game. She wasn't physically eliminating competitors; she was distracting them, planting a thought in their minds, making them lose focus at the worst possible moment. It was so simple, just brilliant.

Nuro advanced toward her, prepared. The moment he was within earshot, she turned slightly, her lips parting just enough to say: *"Watch out for your feet."*

Nuro grinned. *"That trick won't work on me. Try another one."*

A flicker of amusement crossed her face.

"Clever."

Then, after a pause, she studied him.

"But you're not that good at skimming on water," she added, tilting her head slightly. *"I think my horse does it better than you."*

Nuro laughed under his breath, *"then show me how it's done better."*

The girl raised a brow, considering him. Then, finally, she said,

"It's all about surface tension. The more surface area your foot has with the water, the more stable you'll be. That's it."

She glanced at him, then continued,

"Don't start by touching the water with your forefoot— that's how you slip. Put your foot down flat, all at once. Balance comes from spreading the tension across the surface."

"And, of course, never let both feet touch the water simultaneously. Do that, and you'll skim uncontrollably."

Nuro nodded, processing the advice. Then, carefully, he adjusted his footing, trying to apply her technique. Ahead, the end of the competition loomed closer. By now, most competitors have fallen. Only a handful remained.

Then, from the side, a girl with an elongated neck like a giraffe moved toward Nuro, stepping into his path. Her intention was clear—to throw him off balance. Nuro, quick on his feet, sidestepped smoothly, facing her with a raised brow.

His gaze flickered to the metal rings around her neck.

"What's with those rings?" he asked.

Then, in broken English, she replied, *"Dzilla... nefer heard tat befour?"*

Nuro smirked. *"Nope."*

The Dzilla girl frowned. *"You did understood me? Is my English bad? Understood me?"*

Nuro didn't miss a beat. With a casual flick of his hand, he pointed at her feet.

"Watch your step."

She blinked, confused. Then, instinctively, she looked down. That single glance was all it took.

Her foot slipped, her body wavered, and within seconds, she tumbled backward, plunging into the water with a loud splash.

As she fell, Nuro's gaze lingered on the golden rings around her neck, watching as they sank beneath the surface. After the rings disappeared under the water, he grinned, stepping past the ripples where she had fallen.

Now, only three competitors remained: Buffalo-eyed girl, Nuro, and, of course, Kato—still skimming on his belly.

The far shore loomed ahead. The buffalo-eyed girl inhaled deeply, then burst forward. Nuro matched her pace instantly. Their steps quickened, their feet barely making contact with the water, skimming faster and faster. They were neck to neck, both determined to finish first.

Behind them, the Dzilla girl had resurfaced, coughing, soaked, and furious. She squinted toward the front of the race, trying to see who would win.

On the other side of the lake, Fahd stood waiting. When he saw Kato still skimming on his belly, he sighed and tossed out a rope.

"Grab on!"

Kato finally managed to roll onto his back, his face half-submerged as he groaned. He reached for the rope, grabbing it with both hands. Fahd pulled him across the remaining distance, dragging him like a makeshift raft. Kato grumbled the entire way.

Back in the race, the Dzilla girl was desperate to see the winner. She moved through the water, searching for a better vantage point, her eyes flicking between Nuro and the buffalo-eyed girl.

Finally, she spotted a stone near the surface. She stepped onto it, jumping to elevate herself, but her foot slipped. Again. She splashed back into the water just as—The horn blasted.

On land, Nuro stood, catching his breath. Then, across the shore, his gaze met hers. The buffalo-eyed girl held his stare, her face calm. Then, a subtle, knowing smile.

While all of Orun was preparing for the grand *Mvua* ceremony, Okasha asked Chad to stand for him at a summit with the leaders of Barzakh, who were also attending the celebration. It was a regular meeting to discuss food chain transfers, Crossers' regulations, and border agreements.

But today, something was different. As the meeting began, the generals of Barzakh greeted Chad with unusual reverence.

"Majesty, King Okasha,*"* one of them said, his voice thick with formality. *"We are truly honored to meet you, especially on this great day of celebration."*

For a moment, Chad froze. The title caught him off guard. Then, realizing the misunderstanding, he straightened his posture and cleared his throat.

"I'm sorry, generals," he said, trying to hide his discomfort.

"I am not King Okasha. I'm his son, Chad."

A brief pause. One of the generals quickly adjusted his tone.

"Ah, then Crown Prince Chad."

Chad's jaw tightened. But just for a moment...he liked it. No one had been officially named Crown Prince. Not yet. Still, he didn't correct them. He let it linger. Swallowed it with quiet pleasure.

The generals nodded and smoothly returned to the agenda, border regulations, and ongoing concerns about the food chain.

Okasha's family stood prepared for the ceremony, *the Mvua*. Their expressions were solemn, yet expectant. All except Chad. Nuro spotted him from afar, walking toward them, clearly returning from his meeting. Beside Nuro, Kato remained silent. His clothes were still damp, his posture was tense, as if he had been waiting for an apology that never came. Nuro said nothing.

They each raised their own clay cups, filled with water. Then, one by one, they added a few drops of Gravitron fluid to their cups. The water shimmered softly as the liquid mixed in.

Then, they waited. Each Orunian summoned a wish, a dream, a silent plea whispered within.

For a few seconds, the only sound was the soft rustling of robes against the evening breeze.

Then, the horn blasted.

As one, thousands of hands thrust their cups skyward. What followed was nothing short of magic. The drops of water detached, rising instead of falling. Like a gift returned, the sky welcomed back its own rain, reversing its natural course.

From a distance, it looked as if the entire kingdom had inverted, as if the heavens themselves had turned upside down. Water ascended, drifting higher and higher.

And in that extraordinary, weightless moment, Nuro wasn't watching.

His cup had been raised, his hands had followed tradition—but his eyes had not. His gaze remained locked on the buffalo-eyed girl. She was aware of it. She knew even as she participated, and the water rose from her hands.

Yet, she acted as if she hadn't noticed. She did not look back. She did not acknowledge him. She simply let the rain rise.

After *Mvua*, the great event of the day had arrived. The moment everyone had been waiting for.

Behind Chad, his loyal soldiers—the Ray Riders—stood ready. Prepared to lift him high into the sky, the moment his name was called. Because everyone knew who Chad was, the greatest Stingray Rider in the kingdom—the only one among his brothers groomed for this moment.

The three brothers stood to Okasha's left, Chad positioned closest to him. On the opposite side, their mother, Amara, and the eight tribal leaders stood in quiet observation.

Among them, the leader of the Amázigh tribe studied Chad intently. He had known Chad since childhood. He remembered that day after the WAOFO attacks, when Chad had stood behind Okasha, mirroring his posture, his young face etched with determination. That was the day the Amázigh leader had believed Chad was destined to follow Okasha.

Kato wasn't paying attention. He stood beside his brothers, but his mind was elsewhere. Inside his pocket, his fingers twitched, tapping patterns invisible to others. Nuro glanced at him, narrowing his eyes.

The Bug Thread. A neural patch hidden behind Kato's ear. He wasn't silent like the rest; he was playing in a virtual world. Nuro frowned but said nothing.

Across from them, Okasha lifted the anointing horn into the air. The moment had come. All eyes locked onto him. Kato was still distracted.

Okasha's voice boomed through the crowds.

"Orun *Daima!*"

The crowd erupted in unison.

"Orun *Daima!* Orun *Daima!*"

Okasha stepped forward. Then, he turned left.

The oil poured.

But not over Chad.

Over Fahd. Time stopped.

The only movement was the oil, slipping down Fahd's hair, tracing the curve of his face, soaking into his tunic. Everything else—still.

Chad's smile, frozen in place. The Ray-Riders behind him, waiting to lift him into the sky, stunned, unmoving. Even Kato, lost in his own world moments ago, had stopped. For a brief moment, nothing made sense. The moment dragged endlessly, suffocating in its silence.

Then, the first thought that jumped into Chad's mind. The Barzakh leaders. Just earlier, they had addressed him as Crown Prince Chad. He hadn't corrected them. He had let it linger, swallowing it with pleasure. And now—he wished he had. Now, in their eyes, he would be the fool who lost everything in a single moment.

Something had to happen to make the frozen bodies move again. As not expected, Chad moved the stagnant water.

Without hesitation, he grabbed a wooden staff and struck it against the ground. The sharp echo cracked through the silence.

One beat.

Then another. A signal. A show of support.

The three brothers stared at the ground, none of them daring to meet each other's eyes. Even Fahd, who had just been anointed, refused to look at Chad. Instead, he busied himself wiping the oil from his face, as if that simple act would shield him from the weight of what had just happened.

The Ray-Riders hesitated. They had stood behind Chad all day. Now, he wasn't the Crown Prince. Their purpose was lost. Should they stand behind Fahd instead? Should they lift him into the sky as tradition demanded? Would it be a humiliation to Chad? They exchanged uncertain glances.

Then, one by one, they started to disperse. Chad watched them go.

Amara was stunned. Okasha had never told her. She had always believed Chad would be named Crown Prince. He was the military son, the one who had prepared for this day since childhood. Her mind raced, but she saw no trace of emotion on Chad's face.

And then, Chad stepped forward. He placed a hand on Fahd's shoulder.

"We are brothers," he said. *"Always, in soul and blood."*

Nuro exhaled deeply. For a moment, he had feared Chad would react differently. Then, the frozen silence melted.

The crowd erupted.

"Fahd! Fahd! Fahd! Fahd!"

Chad joined them.

"Fahd. Fahd. Fahd. "

But then, something changed. A noise pierced his head. Not from the crowd—inside his own skull.

A sharp, endless ringing.

F-f-f-f-f-f-f-f-f.

His hands shot up to his ears, trying to stop the chaos inside his skull. Inside—the piercing tinnitus, an endless ringing tearing through his head. Outside—the deafening chants, a mixture of noise triggering an explosion. He gritted his teeth, pressing his palms against his head.

The sound wouldn't stop. He wanted to scream,

"Shut. Up. All of you." But he didn't.

Instead, he turned to Kato.

"Loan me your Bug Thread."

"What?" Kato, still caught in the celebration, blinked at him.

"Just give it to me!" Chad snapped.

Kato hesitated, then peeled the Bug Thread from behind his ear and handed it over. Chad slapped it onto his skin. The device activated instantly. Music filled his head. The tinnitus vanished. The crowd's voices were muted.

The day was ending. The last of the Orunians and tribal leaders had left, their voices fading into the distance. But Nuro stayed. He searched for her. He barely knew her name, yet he felt an unexplainable pull toward her. He searched everywhere but found no trace.

Still, he waited.

Something in him refused to leave. As darkness settled over, he stood alone, his horse by his side, ready to depart.

Then, a sound. A distant horse's call.

Nuro noticed a dim light flickering between two distant peaks, on the right side of Orun's Lake. Curious, he climbed up there and found himself caught between clusters of trees and tall savanna grasses.

Then, he saw it.

A path, narrow and winding, tucked between two enormous trees. Unlike the land around it, this path was clear of grass. The ground was exposed, dusty, stony, and wild. It curved upward. He took it.

The slope was too steep for his horse, so he dismounted, placed one hand on the reins, and began to climb on foot. Step by step. The path rose and fell like a wave, dipping low before rising again.

And then, he saw her. The girl with buffalo eyes. Only her buffalo eyes were visible, gleaming like distant stars. Her skin was dark as the earth, no, even darker.

She sat on a low plateau, a quiet plain carved between the hills. The savanna grasses didn't reach this far. The ground here was soft and simple, covered in short green tufts, as if nature itself had cleared a space just for her.

As he stepped closer, he stopped to take in the sight.

On either side of her, the two mountains stood tall, silent, timeless, like ancient guards watching over the place. In the darkness, she sat alone, her gaze fixed on Orun's city below.

Nuro hesitated. Then, with a deep breath, he straightened his posture and approached.

"Hey there," he said, his voice steady but unsure.

She turned slightly, listening.

>*"What a beautiful place you have here,"* he said.

>*"It's... peaceful."*

The girl smiled softly.

>*"It's my heaven. My hidden heaven."*

She paused.

>*"No one knows about it. No one. Except now... you."*

Then, she looked down at the grass beneath her feet.

"When I'm sad or need to listen to myself, I come here. So... I hope it stays a secret."

She glanced up at him again, her voice quiet, serious.

"A secret between us. Agreed?"

>Nuro nodded. *"Sure. I also wanted to congratulate you. You deserved to win the race. I didn't really have the chance earlier."*

A pause. Then, she tilted her head.

"Thanks. Appreciate that," she said. Then, with a teasing smirk, *"But still... my horse could do it better than you."*

Nuro burst into laughter. Then, shaking his head, he asked, *"I don't even know your name."*

"Taziri."

"From?"

"Amázigh."

"I'm Nuro.*"*

They shook hands.

Nuro studied her. *"Taziri... that's a rare name. I've never heard it before."*

"It means the full moon." She looked back toward Orun. *"My mother chose it for me."*

Nuro leaned slightly forward. *"We don't have the moon anymore. I guess your mother saw it before it vanished. But neither of us did."*

Taziri replied softly, *"But I'm sure you did... the moon."*

Nuro's face twisted in confusion, as if her meaning had slipped right past him. Taziri smirked, then asked him to look into her eyes.

Nuro hesitated. His heartbeat quickened, but he did as she asked. Her buffalo eyes reflected the faint glow of the *Lune* hanging in the sky.

She smiled. *"Tell me what you see."*

Nuro swallowed. *"Your eyes."*

Taziri shook her head. *"And?"* She raised her hand, gesturing gently, urging him to think. But still, he didn't get it.

She sighed, then pointed upward.

> *"Look at the sky. What do you see?"*

Nuro followed her gaze, scratched the back of his head, *"The Lune."*

> *"Now, look again into my eyes."*

And then, he saw it. The glowing circle of the artificial moon reflected perfectly in her irises. His breath hitched.

> *"It's the Lune—the rings. You have lunar eyes,"* he
> murmured. *"The moon… inside your eyes."*

Taziri's smile widened slightly.

"Ahh, finally." Then, with a playful smirk, she added, *"But listen—I have eyes up in the sky. I watch everything. So don't mess around."*

> *"Even in the darkness?"* he teased.

She let the moment hang in the air, then chuckled. *"Even… Your eyes and teeth will always betray you."*

He sighed dramatically. *"Ahh, those traitors… It's always them. Unfortunately, I can't turn them black."*

They laughed together.

Suddenly, Taziri's horse pinned his ears back, pawing at the ground. His posture stiffened, his body angled slightly between them. Taziri sighed. She walked toward him, placing a gentle hand on his neck.

"It's alright," she whispered, stroking his mane. *"Nuro is a friend."*

The horse shook his head in protest. Taziri laughed.

Nuro raised a brow. *"Everything alright?"*

Taziri sighed again. *"I hope.... He's jealous. He's never reacted like this before... never."*

She turned back to Nuro. *"Tell me, what's your brain dream, Nuro?"*

Nuro frowned. *"Brain dream?"*

"The deepest wish you have... What did you wish for today—at Mvua—when you rained the sky?"

Nuro let out a slow breath.

"For me," Nuro said, *"there are many things I just don't believe in.*

Why are we even 'raining' the sky? It probably doesn't even need it. What can a few drops of water mixed with Gravitron really do? This whole ceremony is only Tales of our ancestors.

We're just repeating what our ancestors did and believed, chasing shadows. Nothing more. Like the

*second sun, the twin, people still think it's real,
something divine. But it's just a reflection—a mirage
caused by radiation.*

And yet, Orunians *still believe we have twin suns…"*

Taziri's expression shifted. For the first time, she looked disappointed.

"I'm a believer, Nuro," she said softly. *"I believe in
Mvua, and in those ancient myths."*

Nuro didn't respond. A silence settled between them. Then, the soft hiss of a mechanical pump.

Taziri's eyes flicked down to Nuro's belt, where a small device was attached, emitting a rhythmic pulse. Her curiosity got the better of her. *"Can I ask… what is that?"*

Nuro glanced at it briefly. *"Genetic medication. I've been
receiving it since birth. The pump administers constant doses."*

Taziri studied him for a moment. *"So… does your name
have meaning?"*

Nuro nodded. *"It means 'light'. And if you reverse it… Orun."*

Suddenly, her horse tugged against his rope, kicking the tree it was tied to.

Taziri sighed. *"I think I have to go. My horse isn't letting me
stay any longer."* She stepped into the saddle, adjusting her grip on the reins. *"I love him,"* she said simply. *"He's my family."*

She turned to leave. *"Bye,* Nuro.*"* Her horse took a few steps forward.

"Wait, wait!" Nuro called after her.

She paused, glancing back over her shoulder. For a moment, she thought he would ask to see her again. Instead, he grinned. *"Would you loan me some of your Gravitron? I don't have any left."*

Taziri laughed in disbelief. *"It's karma,"* she teased. *"I saw you give yours away to your brother."* She smirked, shook her head, then kicked her horse into a run, skimming across Orun's lake to the other side.

Nuro stood there, watching. He was frustrated. Now, he had to take the long path through the mountains to get home. It would take hours. Taziri was gone. The sound of her horse's hooves had long faded into the night. Nuro stood alone, watching the spot where she had vanished. Then, he noticed something.

She had forgotten her bag. He picked it up from the ground, his fingers tracing the fabric, which had rough edges but was finely crafted.

He smiled. At that moment, he knew he would see her again. His smile lingered until his horse grumbled lowly, then struck the ground with its hoof. Nuro glanced up, his expression shifting. His horse had noticed that his rider's thoughts were not on the journey ahead, but on the bag's owner.

Nuro sighed, slinging the bag over his shoulder before mounting his horse.

"Alright, alright. Let's go." The journey began in silence. The horse's steps echoed softly against the winding mountain paths, moving steadily around Orun's great lake. Nuro's grip on the reins relaxed. The rhythm of the ride, the night air cooling his skin, the distant water stretching endlessly beside him, His eyelids grew heavy.

Slowly...He drifted. The horse stopped abruptly. A deep, low grumble rumbled from its chest. Nuro's eyes snapped open. For a moment, he was disoriented. He straightened, blinking away the haze of sleep.

"What's wrong?" he murmured, patting the horse's side. But the horse didn't move. Its ears twitched, its posture tense. Nuro climbed down, gripping the reins as he scanned the darkness ahead. Then, he heard it.

A distant yet unmistakable sound comes from the far end of the plateau—a deep, rhythmic roar. It is not the sound of wind or the rustling of trees, it is something else.

Nuro stepped forward, following the sound. As he walked, the air thickened, saturated with moisture. A fine mist clung to his skin, leaving his clothes damp and heavy. The closer he got, the harder it became to see. His breath hitched. The smell of fresh earth filled his lungs. The sound grew louder.

He wiped his hands over his arms, which were wet. But something was… wrong. The droplets were running upward, upward toward the sky!

Nuro locked in place. Gravitron? He took another step forward. Then, he gasped. His foot nearly slipped off the edge. He had almost walked straight into a cliff. But that wasn't what made his breath catch in his throat. Before him—the waterfall.

But it was falling upwards, straight into the sky. Nuro stood frozen, unable to tear his eyes away. The water defied gravity, rushing toward the heavens, as if the sky itself was drinking from the Earth. He had never seen anything like it.

A natural wonder? A phenomenon of Gravitron?

Or a sign?

His first instinct was to take some of the Gravitron. If he could collect it and give it to his horse, he could skim across the lake effortlessly. He reached for his flask. But then, Taziri's voice echoed in his mind.

"I am a believer, Nuro. I believe in Mvua, and in those ancient myths." His hand stopped.

For the first time, he thought about his own Unabii, which had repeated itself dozens of times since birth.

Why? What if Taziri was right? What if Unabii was not just a cycle of subconscious dreams? What if it were real?

Nuro's jaw tightened. He had always dismissed *Mvua* as an illusion, never believing in Unabiis or in Siddiq's teachings.

But what if I was wrong? He took a slow breath. *"Are we, as Humans, truly free?"* Or *was everything predestined? If so, then... What was the point of knowing one's destiny—if it could never be changed?*

The thought weighed on him. Then, a decision. Turned back toward his horse. And whispered, *"Let's shoot down my Unabii."*

By the time Nuro reached Siddiq's home, he had descended into the valley behind Orun's lake. The first sun had already risen. The door was open. Nuro slowed his horse, eyes narrowing as he noticed a figure inside, a woman, sitting on the floor.

His steps halted. His instinct told him to turn away. Lowering his gaze, he stepped back and retreated toward his horse, his fingers absentmindedly brushing against the reins.

He would wait. Siddiq wasn't inside. Nuro turned his head and spotted him outside, kneeling in prayer behind a large palm tree. He stood still, waiting, allowing the old man his moment of worship.

The prayer ended. Siddiq rose to his feet, dusted off his robe, and turned toward Nuro. For a brief second, their eyes met. Nuro expected a greeting, a nod, a glance, a single word. But Siddiq said nothing. He simply walked past Nuro, entered his home, and closed the door behind him. Nuro stood frozen, stunned.

His mind reeled. *He isn't blind enough not to see me...So why had he ignored him?*

Was it personal? Had I done something wrong?

Thoughts clawed at him, but another feeling quickly replaced them: curiosity. His gaze flickered back to the half-open window. He hesitated. It wasn't his nature to spy, but his curiosity was unbearable.

Just for a second, he stole a glance. The woman remained seated, her back turned. Then, Siddiq approached her. He placed his hands over her head. She shook. As if she were crying, the woman remained seated, her back to him. He couldn't see her face.

But then, his breath caught. The turban on her head... He knew it. His heartbeat quickened. He knew the woman inside. He tried to shift his position, peering from another angle, but all he could see was the turban. He clenched his jaw. He would wait. He had to until she came out.

Meanwhile, outside Siddiq's home, Nuro waited. But elsewhere, Chad was fighting a different battle. The chaos inside his skull was relentless. The Bug behind his ear, his one escape, was useless now. The noise grew louder, heavier, unbearable.

His skull felt like it was splitting apart, the migraine sawing through his brain in jagged pieces. He clutched his head, pressing his palms against his ears to contain the storm inside.

Even the music, his last refuge, was worthless now. He increased the volume, higher, higher, but the noise only grew louder. It was deafening.

Then, *"Shut up!"*

He screamed, his voice raw, a desperate roar against the invisible war raging inside him. But the ringing never stopped. For a fleeting second, the pressure inside him eased. The scream had helped. It was a release. He sat at the edge of his bed and slowly removed the Bug behind his ear.

He would face the voices head-on. Chad never lost a battle. He never surrendered. He was the Stingray-Rider.

Stretching his body across the bed, he closed his eyes. And within seconds, he fell asleep. Then, air stirred against his right ear.

A presence.

A whisper.

"Kill him."

"Kill him."

A woman's voice. Chad jerked upright. He stood on his bed, scanning the room, his pulse pounding. The whisper had been real. It wasn't inside his head. It had been right beside him.

His breath shook. His fingers reached behind his ear; *had he forgotten to remove the Bug?* But no, it was already off. And yet...He had heard it.

He had felt the warmth of breath against his skin. He was sure. Then, his eyes locked onto his door. Something was hanging on it.

A shiny present.

Chad rubbed his face firmly, shut his eyes briefly, then opened them again. No. He wasn't hallucinating. The object was still there. He climbed down from his bed, his steps slow and deliberate.

Now, he was standing right in front of it. His eyes fixed on it.

A sword.

He grasped it. It was heavy and cold. The blade was rusted, and its edge had eroded over time.

But at its golden base, an engraving gleamed under the dim light.

CHAD.

His sword!.

But how had it gotten here? His grip tightened. He turned it over and brushed the rust off the blade. And there, etched into the steel, another name.

NURO.

His brother. Chad's pulse thundered.

Who had brought this sword here? Who had left it inside my room, in the moment I had fallen asleep? The person must still be close.

With a sharp movement, he flung the door open. He stepped forward, sword in hand, and then stopped. Outside the door was no longer his home. He was standing on a plateau. He looked around. He knew this place, but it was miles away from home. He turned back. His door was still there, standing alone, closed behind him.

Ahead—A burning sun hung low in the sky. It was massive, golden, solitary. Chad could look directly at it without blinking. He walked forward. With each step, the sun grew smaller, lower. And he grew larger.

He was greater. He was stronger.

He stood before the sun, one arm's length away. It was now below his chest level.

The sun feared him. Then, clouds appeared—eight dark clouds creeping from behind the sun, surrounding it and defending it. They sensed the sun's fear. They had come to protect it.

Chad's jaw tightened. His grip hardened around the sword. A surge of rage swelled inside him.

He yelled, raised his sword, and with two brutal swings—He shattered the eight clouds into nothing. They vanished. Then, the sun disappeared.

Now it is Darkness.

And from behind it, a pale light emerged. A globe, illuminating white. It gave off a quiet, weak glow. It was the moon. Chad's breath came faster. Rage coiled inside him.

The moon!

It had been destroyed long ago. It should not be here.

He raised his sword again. With one mighty swing—He split the moon in two. It was still glowing, barely. He saw its weakness.

He lifted his sword high into the sky, its sharp end pointing upward, as if he could stab the heavens themselves.

Then, the scent. A familiar, metallic tang. Rust.

His fingers brushed against his face. Something warm dripped onto his forehead. He wiped his hand over his skin and looked down.

Blood.

His hands. Covered. He looked around, his feet had disappeared. A pool of blood surrounded him. It was everywhere. Then, he looked up.

The sky was bleeding. A rain of blood poured down, drenching his skin, his clothes, his sword. Chad opened his mouth, tasting it. But it wasn't enough. He bent down, cupped his hands, filled them with blood, and drank. The warmth slid down his throat. He wiped the excess from the corner of his mouth.

Then, He roared into the sky.

"I AM THE GREATEST!"

"I AM THE VICTORIOUS!"

His sword raised high once more. Then, he lowered it. The battle was over. He turned back toward his door. He stepped into his room. His body was soaked in blood. He placed the victorious sword beneath his bed. He removed his clothes, bloodied beyond recognition: his hands, his arms, his chest, all stained red. But there was no time to rest. It was midday. He had meetings to attend. And so, he prepared, as if nothing had happened.

Nuro was still waiting outside Siddiq's home. The twin suns had already risen, their light casting long shadows over the small house.

Yet, the woman inside still hadn't come out. Impatience gnawed at him. He glanced again through the window. The curtain's soft sway blurred his view, but the woman in the familiar turban remained seated.

He shifted, angling himself for a clearer view. Then, between the swinging fabric, he saw it. A vein on the side of her face. It only appeared when she was emotional. His breath caught again. The woman turned toward the window.

Amara. His mother.

Panic shot through him. Without thinking, his body dropped to the ground.

Did she see me? His heart sank the moment his body dropped to the ground, barely breathing. Seconds passed. He didn't wait to find out. Dragging himself backward, he reached for his horse, untied the reins in a rush, and rode away.

As he rode, Nuro's thoughts spiraled: *That was my mother. I should have stayed. I should have knocked. But instead—I crawled away like a thief.* His grip tightened on the reins. *Maybe it would have been wiser to wait outside. To meet her. To face her. But now, it was too late.*

Unabii

Okasha was waiting for Amara. He sat at his throne table, his body wrapped in the heavy folds of his royal Isiagu robes. But— he couldn't remember how he got here.

Where was I before this? His mind searched for a memory, a clue—but nothing.

Only emptiness.

Before him lay a map of Orun, spread across the table. Drops of water splashed onto its surface.

The ink blurred, bleeding at the edges, dissolving the kingdom's borders. The falling drops quickened, one after another. Okasha's breath hitched. Then, realization.

It was not water. It was his own sweat.

His clothes were too heavy. The weight is unbearable. His chest struggled against the weight, fighting for air. The trapped air inside him fought for release, his lungs wheezing like a kettle on the verge of boiling.

His fingers clawed at his collar, trying to loosen it. He could barely breathe. Neck veins bulged against his skin. His vision swam. His hands finally undid the top button of his robe, just enough to win a few shallow breaths. But it was too late. The heaviness in his chest surged again.

His lungs collapsed inward, forcing out a final ragged gasp. His body gave out.

He crashed forward, his forehead slamming onto the table. The weight of his crown followed, tumbling off his head, rolling across the eroded map.

Then, it fell to the ground.

Foam seeped from his mouth, spreading across the undissolved parts of Orun's map. The last uncharted land swallowed. His chest stopped rising. His eyes turned upward. His vision darkened.

"Okasha... Okasha!" A voice pierced through the void.

The voice shook him. Okasha's eyes snapped open. His vision blurred.

Amara stood before him. He tried to speak, to tell her what was happening—but his mouth was locked. He fought to make a noise. A muffled, strangled cry slipped out.

Amara frowned. She couldn't understand him.

He tried again, but still, only silence. Hopeless, he thrashed against the invisible force holding him still. His hands shot up, grasping at something, her pearl necklace.

The chain snapped under the force of his pull. Four pearls spilled onto the floor. They rolled, one after another.

Okasha's eyes followed their path, locked on them.

Then, he blinked. Amara was gone. Vanished.

The pearls continued rolling toward the exit door.

His body collapsed onto the ground, landing hard on his hands. The world spun around him. His vision flickered.

But he had one goal—the pearls.

He crawled toward them, inch by inch. They had to be collected again and brought back together like a chain.

The exit door stood before him. But the pearls were gone. Everything he had done, evaporated. Okasha's mind shuddered as he turned his head. A figure stood nearby.

A man.

Okasha's eyes fell to his shoes. He knew those shoes. This man could save the pearls. Okasha looked up.

The man was smiling. A smile as calm as an angel. And Okasha knew him. His grandfather. A man who had died decades ago. Something was wrong.

Am I dreaming? But this felt real. Too real.

If it were a dream—I can stand again. I can breathe.

It had to be an illusion. Yet, his body did not move. His chest remained tight. He struggled to understand.

His grandfather stood as he had in his youth, young, no older than thirty, with the same smile and the same posture, as if no time had passed.

Okasha forced the words from his throat.

"Are you happy?"

The dead man did not answer.

Okasha swallowed.

"Tell me about life after death."

Nothing.

Okasha asked again. *"Are you in heaven?"*

His grandfather only smiled; his hand extended. Okasha hesitated. Then he took it and stepped through the exit door. Together, they passed.

##

Amara had just returned home from her visit to Siddiq. Okasha was still asleep. Drenched in sweat. He was breathing steadily, no longer gasping for air.

"Okasha…"

Her voice was soft, but he heard her. His body, which had felt paralyzed, could move again. His chest is no longer heavy. His lungs no longer fought for air.

He whispered her name. *"Amara."*

She pressed her palm against his forehead. He was warm. Too warm. He reached for her hand, lifted it to his lips, and kissed her palm. Slowly, he sat upright on the bed. She was beside him, close enough to feel his body trembling. Okasha couldn't stop shaking.

"It's cold," he murmured. *"Too cold... cover me."*

Amara reached for a blanket, wrapping it around him. But it wasn't enough. His body still shuddered uncontrollably. She removed the warm scarf from around her neck and placed it over his shoulders.

Still, he trembled.

She took off her turban, covering his damp forehead. The shaking slowed. The weight in his chest eased.

Okasha exhaled, voice low. *"You are my warmth."*

Amara moved closer and kissed his forehead. *"Tell me, my moon... do you feel ill?"*

She glanced at his soaked bedsheets. *"It looks like you've been wrestling demons in your sleep."* Okasha met her gaze but said nothing. She knew him too well. Even when he was silent, his eyes spoke.

"You want to tell me something, don't you?" she asked. *"I can see it in your face."*

Okasha lowered his gaze.

Amara hesitated. She had returned home with a truth—urgent and heavy. Something critical. Something he needed to know. But now... she hesitated. Then, she saw it.

His eyes narrowed slightly, a sharp glint forming in them. A small movement. A flicker. His eyes shone, blinking rapidly, as if trying to hold something back. Then Okasha collapsed into her arms. His head fell onto her chest. She placed her hand over his head, gently stroking his damp hair.

For the first time in her life, she saw her husband cry. She had never seen him like this. He had always been unshakable. But now, he was breaking.

She smiled softly, as if to calm him, but inside, she felt something else, a deep fear that made her stomach tighten. She wiped the tears from his face, saying nothing.

Then, she kissed his eyes. She waited.

She just watched him, smiling softly, waiting.

Okasha finally spoke. *"I had an Unabii."*

Amara's eyes widened slightly. She had not expected this. This was precisely what she had wanted to tell him.

Okasha's voice was low, steady.

"It wasn't a pleasant one."

Amara listened.

"I lost Orun. *You vanished. Then my grandfather took me. We passed through the exit door together."*

She inhaled sharply. *"Did you follow him?"*

Okasha nodded. *"Yes. I followed him. We both passed through the exit door."*

Amara's stomach clenched. She remembered her grandmother's warning. She had told her this when Amara was a child...

If you follow a dead family member in an Unabii...

It means you will pass soon.

Her fingers curled slightly. She forced herself to remain calm. *"But you don't know if it was an Unabii or just a dream,"* she said.

Okasha shook his head.

> *"Look at my bed. Look at me. I was drowning in my own sweat. You saw how I was shaking when you woke me up."*

She couldn't argue. But she tried. *"Then wait. If it comes again, you will know for sure."*

Okasha's voice hardened.

"There is no time to wait. It must be shot down now. I must see Siddiq."

Amara knew she had lost the moment. Her secret—the one she had come home prepared to tell him—She would bury it for now. He was too shaken. Too vulnerable. He wasn't ready for more.

Okasha stood up. Began preparing himself. She watched him silently. His movements felt different, as if a part of him was already gone. Okasha couldn't wait any longer. After preparing himself, he left for Siddiq's home.

The door was open. He knocked. No answer. Stepping inside, he immediately noticed the simplicity of the place. Only two rooms. No chairs. Just a straw mat on the ground. He scanned the space, but Siddiq wasn't there.

He would have to wait. With no other option, he lowered himself to the ground, leaning his back against the wall. His eyes drifted upward. The roof, woven from palm branches, let in streams of golden light; in them, tiny dust particles floated, suspended in the silence.

Through the window, he finally saw him. Siddiq stood outside, behind a palm tree. The curtain swayed, obscuring his view, then revealing it again. Siddiq was seated now, his hands raised toward the sky. He was speaking to the Creator.

Okasha's right leg began to shake. It only happened when he was under stress. He looked again through the window. Still, Siddiq hadn't finished praying.

The shaking in his leg grew worse, almost as if he were having a seizure. Then, Siddiq entered the house. Okasha's leg stilled as he quickly stood up, opening his arms in greeting.

But Siddiq walked right past him. He moved toward the window, closed it, and continued as if Okasha weren't even there.

The same thing had happened to his son, Nuro, not long ago. Okasha cleared his throat, forcing a slight cough to break the silence. Still, Siddiq said nothing.

For a brief moment, Okasha had a thought. *"He's not so blind that he can't see me standing before him."*

Then, Siddiq finally spoke.

"Insight for a blind heart is greater than sight for a blind eye."

Okasha's mind stalled. Had he just read his thoughts? He hadn't spoken a single word. Shock rippled through him. Siddiq stood calmly, Okasha exhaled. *"Our* Siddiq, *it's me,* Okasha. *Your servant. I seek your wisdom."*

Siddiq listened in silence. Okasha told him everything. Every detail of his Unabii—up to the moment he stepped through the exit door with his grandfather. Siddiq absorbed each word. Then, finally, he spoke.

"Son, the destiny of the Creator is like an arrow. It is released behind you the moment you're born.

So—run run run.

Run like a beast.

Run like prey.

Be faster than the arrow.

But time... age...both will weaken you...

They will steal your breath.

Slow your steps.

Even if you escape, even if you hide.

In the end.

The arrow will catch you.

So, it is with the destiny of our Creator."

Then, he continued.

"The map in your Unabii is your life—eroding."

"Orun is your son, Nuro. *But in the Unabii, it was reversed."*

"The crown is your kingdom. Nuro *will take it—but only briefly."*

"The four pearls are great trials you will face."

"The necklace is your sons—its chain is their unity. But that unity will be lost."

"Your grandfather waits to take your hand—to his world."

Then, Siddiq stopped.

Okasha's eyes narrowed. *"And* Amara?*"*

Siddiq said nothing.

Okasha *leaned in, his voice tense.* "Amara *vanished in my Unabii. I told you that, didn't I?"*

Siddiq only smiled. A smile that held something back. Then, he stood. *"Come. Take me outside."*

Okasha hesitated, then helped him up, holding his arm for support. As they stepped outside, Siddiq handed Okasha his staff.

"Draw a circle around your feet," he said. Okasha obeyed, tracing a perfect circle in the dust.

"This is your life. The circle. It is limited. It has boundaries."
Then he raised his hand, gesturing beyond the line.

"Outside of this circle, too, is life. But eternal. Without limits. Without borders. That is freedom."

Siddiq looked at him. *"You must step out to see that you always stood on a limited ground. Death is only a step."*

Okasha felt the weight of those words settle deep within him. Siddiq had calmed him. Or had he simply distracted him?

Okasha sighed. *"Siddiq, my offer still stands. Come to the city. Stay in a bigger home. You need only accept."*

Siddiq simply smiled. *"I am happy with my home."*

Okasha nodded, then lifted Siddiq's staff to hand it back to him. But Siddiq did not move. He did not extend his hands.

Okasha hesitated. *"Siddiq?"* A long silence. He stood there, still, unmoving.

A thought flickered in Okasha's mind. He waved a hand gently in front of Siddiq's eyes. No reaction.

Siddiq is blind.

His earlier words rang in his mind: *"Insight for a blind heart is greater than sight for a blind eye."*

Then Okasha placed the staff directly into Siddiq's hand. Then, quietly, he turned back toward his horse. As he rode away, the calmness of the moment slowly folded over him. He tried to see his Unabii as Siddiq had explained it—like a circle. But in his mind, it did not appear as a circle.

He sees himself as a featherless flamingo, standing on one leg—the other broken, stranded on a shrinking island as the waters rise higher and higher. There is no air. He can neither fly nor breathe. And soon, the island will be gone.

At Okasha's home, Amara sat restless, uneasy. Her thoughts were with Siddiq, wondering—had he told her husband the truth?

But Something felt wrong. Okasha should have returned by now, yet he hadn't. She could feel it. Even from a distance. So she went to Siddiq. But Okasha was no longer there.

He had gone to his father. To his ancestors. To the only ones who could not judge him, but he wasn't standing by their graves. The souls of Okasha's ancestors gathered. They stood in silence, watching. The peace of their tomb had been disturbed. Something horrendous was happening. Something they could not stop. The six souls circled the edge of a hole that had not been there before.

A grave.

Shallow. Dark. Cold.

The earth had been torn apart; its insides scattered into a growing mound of dirt. And inside—A desperate descendant, digging like a mole. Digging. Covered in dirt.

On Amara's way to Siddiq, she saw her husband's horse standing before the gate of his family tomb. She went inside. As Amara reached the edge of the grave, the six souls disappeared. She saw her husband. His hands clawed at the earth; his body was soaked in dust and sweat. She didn't speak. Instead, she climbed down. Without hesitation, she lowered herself into the grave. She wrapped her arms around him from behind, her warmth pressing against his shaking body. Her hands clasped around his chest, just below his arms.

Her voice was soft. *"I know... I know..."*

His voice came hoarse, broken.

"I must be prepared...I must be prepared."

His hands stilled. The weight of her arms stopped his body from trembling. Slowly, he let go of the earth. Then he lay himself back, his body sinking into the dirt. His eyes stared upward. The sky felt distant.

He whispered.

"So, this is it."

"This is how it looks."

"A small hole. Beneath the dirt."

Amara laid herself there beside him, feeling him. She closed her eyes for a moment. She would also bury her secret Unabii with her. He would know it soon enough. She turned her head toward him, her forehead pressing gently against his shoulder. Her hand reached for his, fingers intertwining, holding tightly onto what was left.

She whispered. *"Come with me, we need each other. Every second matters."* And for the first time that day, he let himself be pulled away from the grave.

Nuro used the excuse of returning Taziri's bag to meet her again. Days passed. They crossed paths more than once, and slowly something began to grow. It was deeper in Taziri's heart than in Nuro's. She wasn't even aware of it. Her feeling became intense; his remained quiet. Then, **Friday, September 8, 2241**. That night, as the darkness reached its deepest curve, the silence was shattered.

An angry black bull tore through the halls, roaring like thunder, charging forward, unstoppable.

"Nuro! Nuro!"

The beast was Kato. His feet pounded against the floor, knocking over everything in his way. Without slowing, he threw his full weight into Nuro's door. It ripped off its hinges, collapsing onto the floor with a deafening crash. A pressure wave exploded inside the room, as if a bomb had gone off. Nuro didn't wake up.

Kato's voice shook the walls.

"Nuro! Nuro!"

No response. His head was buried beneath two pillows, one below, one above. Kato grabbed the top pillow and flung it across the room. Then, leaning over him, he shouted directly into his ear.

"Nuro! Nuro!"

Still, nothing. Kato didn't wait. He grabbed him, shaking him violently.

"Nuro! Nuro!"

Finally—his eyes fluttered open.

"Yeah... yeah... I'll come..."

Kato wasn't fooled. Nuro was still half-asleep, trapped between dreams and reality. So Kato shook him again. Harder.

And then, the words that cut through everything.

"Your mother is dying."

Nuro's eyes snapped open completely. His body jerked upright. The room blurred around him. His mind wasn't awake yet, but his body was moving.

Kato grasped his arm, pulling him out of bed and into the hall. They walked through the dim corridors, toward her room. The weight of sleep was still clouding his brain, but as they neared the door, his thoughts started catching up.

His voice was hoarse.

"Kato... what happened to our mother?"

Kato's steps didn't slow.

"She has radiation."

"Radiation?"

His voice was sharp now.

"Where did she get radiation from?"

Kato didn't answer. He just walked. Didn't even look at him. Nuro stopped asking.

They reached her door. His brothers stood outside, the healer beside them. Okasha was on the floor, his body folded into itself, his back pressed against the door.

Nuro didn't speak. He felt Something was building behind his eyes. Pain. A pressure. Something pushing, pressing his eyes outside his skull.

He stepped forward into the room. The air was thick. It wasn't silent, but quiet. There were muffled voices outside. The smell of medical herbs and damp cloth clung to every inch of the room. Nuro's gaze drifted forward.

The window.

Something about it felt wrong. Outside, the night was black—blacker than usual. There was nothing beyond it, no distant lights, no sky, no horizon, only the limbs of her favorite guava tree. But they were too close. They pressed against the glass, stretching inward. The guava fruits, usually bright and white, had turned grey.

Unnatural. Something wasn't right. The tree felt alive.

Watching.

Waiting.

Amara lay on her bed. Her face turned away from the door. She didn't look at her collapsed husband outside. She didn't look at the sons who had gathered. Her eyes had only one focus: the window, the demon tree.

The limbs were creeping closer, and the fruit was staring at her—like predators waiting for their prey. Her breathing was slow and shallow. She turned her gaze away from the window, away from the nightmare beyond the glass. Instead, her eyes traced the wooden ceiling beam above her, where cracks branched out like deep wounds—like scars etched across an old, weathered face.

Nuro stepped forward. The scent of herbs thickened. Something was wrong. Even her room wasn't the same.
The colors—grey.
The photos—grey.
Her clothes—grey.
Everything was grey.

The only thing that hadn't changed—was her fear. Nuro felt it. He turned back to the window. The tree had moved. The limbs were closer. Almost inside.

Nuro reached her bedside. He placed a hand on her forehead, brushing her hair back. Her skin was rigid. Cold. His fingers slid down, gently wrapping around her hand.

Still, cold.

He started massaging it, trying to bring warmth back into her. Amara's lips parted. Her voice was weak. Cracked. She whispered.

"We are all one… from one."

Her index finger twitched. Her body was still freezing. Nuro grabbed a blanket and wrapped her tighter.

Still, cold.

He looked at the window again. The tree had moved closer, and the limbs were inside. The grey guavas had turned into demons' heads, hanging from the tree. The room was getting darker and darker.

Amara took a deep inhale. Then, a short, cold exhale.

Nuro kept looking, watching her chest. He waited. He begged for her chest to rise again. Just one more breath. Just one more word.

But nothing. Her chest remained still.

Her eyes were sunken, icteric.

Closed.

Forever....

Nuro didn't move. Not even his head. Only his eyes flicked toward the window.

The demon tree twitched. Its limbs stepped back. The guava fruit—they fell.

Gone.

At the same time, in another dark place, Taziri was alone, in her hidden heaven, her secret place. The place where she met him for the first time at *Homowo* Day. It had become their romantic place, where they used to meet, but today, she had been waiting. Like a fool. For him. For Nuro.

He had suggested it himself. To watch the twin sunrises together, here, where their paths first crossed. But now, it felt humiliating. He hadn't shown up. He hadn't canceled. He did Nothing.

And yet, she had waited. She had spread the mat carefully, just as she imagined it. She had set everything in place. But he never came. For a while, she sat there, staring upward, watching the dim glow of the *Lune* above. She hadn't touched the snacks she had prepared. The mango and the fresh mango juice were always the first he reached for. She had imagined a perfect sunrise with him.

But now, the night was empty.

Slowly, she began gathering everything. The snacks went back into their box. She packed them slowly, like she was trying to hold onto something already lost. Finally, she folded the mat. Her hand hovered over the fabric for a moment longer than needed. Then, she turned to her horse. He stirred as she approached and nudged her gently.

Her horse knew—he always knew—he was the one who truly felt her sadness. Taziri ran her hand over his mane. Then, she stopped.

No.

She wouldn't let the night end like this. Not because of Him...Nuro.

She turned back and unfolded the mat again, this time for herself. She set it in the same place as before, carefully smoothing the fabric.

She unpacked the mango slices, poured herself a glass of juice, and sat down. For the first time that night, the world around her felt different, empty, but hers.

Then, the world shifted. Something felt wrong.

Above her, the *Lune* flickered like a heartbeat out of rhythm. Taziri frowned. She watched the pulsating light, expecting it to be a temporary anomaly. Yet, the flickering continued. This was not normal.

The moment she had claimed for herself vanished for the second time. Her hands tense. Only moments ago, she had been steady, ready to enjoy the mango juice.

Without hesitation, she moved, folded the mat in a rush, and hurriedly packed everything. Her horse shifted restlessly, his body tense. He had felt it too. Taziri swung herself onto his back. Kicked hard into motion, galloped toward the city. She needed to know what was happening.

As the twin suns began their ascent, the sky turned pale gold, not yet warm. Four hours had passed since Amara took her last breath. She lay alone in her room, waiting to be washed and prepared for the burial.

Outside the door, her husband Okasha sat, unmoving. Speechless. He had not left his place since she died. He had not spoken. He had not wept. His sons stood beside him; their eyes clouded with something that wasn't quite grief.

Then, the washerwoman arrived, and her assistant followed. They stepped into the house and met the gaze of Amara's family. And in those eyes, they saw something unsettling, not mourning, not sorrow.

But Fear.

The washerwoman entered the room, glanced at the window, saw the guava tree, and then opened the window. Then turned to Amara's body, pulling the blanket over her face.

And then, she froze. This was not the Amara she knew. The woman before her was different.

Her expression, her skin, the way death sat upon her, Amara was unhappy. She tried to turn Amara onto her side, but she couldn't. Even with the help of her assistant, the body would not move.

The small, delicate body of Amara had become impossibly heavy. A weight neither of them could lift. The washer stood back, exhaling.

"We need help."

She covered Amara's face again and stepped outside. Her gaze fell on the sons, the husband, who were standing like statues.

"We cannot turn her over," she said. *"Who will come inside and help us?"*

No one answered. Okasha did not move. His four sons looked at one another. Their silence was thick with something unspoken. The washer woman's eyes searched them again. The fear was still there.

But fear of what? The demon tree waiting outside the window?

The grey room, there? Or the dead body of their mother, Amara?

The hesitation dragged on. Then, Nuro spoke in a calm, steady voice.

"I will come inside."

As Nuro entered the room, everything changed. The room returned to itself.

The colors reappeared.

The window welcomed brightness again.

The thick herbal scent faded.

They turned to Amara. The washer pulled back the blanket. And—Amara was smiling.

The washerwoman smiled, too, then she spoke softly to Amara herself.

"My Majesty, I've done it—what you asked me before. I understand now."

Nuro's jaw tightened. He did not like this. He did not like the way she spoke to his mother. His dead mother.

The washerwoman turned to him.

"See? She is smiling now. Before you came, she was not. She wanted you here. That is why she smiles."

Nuro said nothing. He didn't believe in these things. He didn't believe in signs.

But now, he smelled something. Not herbs. Something pleasant. Something familiar. His voice was sharp.

"Did you bring rosemary with you?"

The washer only smiled. For a moment, she said nothing.

Then, softly, *"It's her. She brought it from the other life."* She turned back to Amara.

"Sometimes it's basil. Jasmine. Rosemary. And sometimes…"

Her voice lowered.

"Sometimes, it is a foul scent, no matter how tightly you close your nose, it stays inside you for years."

They undressed Amara gently, then lifted her onto the mortuary table and poured pure water over her body. Nuro stood there, watching. His mind drifted, thinking of everything that had changed.

The scent—gone.

The colors—returned.

The room—no longer grey.

It was real. Everything he saw, smelled, and felt. But before he could process it further, the washerwoman interrupted his thoughts. She turned to Amara's body and spoke.

"My Majesty Amara, you are too rigid. I would ask you to relax."

Nuro's voice was sharp.

"She is dead. What are you saying?"

The washer woman's gaze did not waver.

"You saw. You smelled. You experienced it. And still, you do not believe?"

She dipped her hands into the water.

"The dead feel, Nuro, they hear. They understand. They do not move. They do not speak. But they leave things behind, a smell, a movement, a smile."

She glanced at him.

"And every sign you have witnessed... shows that she is happy."

Then, it happened.

Amara's rigid body moved.

Her arms softened.

Her limbs loosened.

She relaxed.

Nuro watched. He said nothing. The washerwoman did not comment. She saw it in his eyes. Sometimes, there is nothing to say. Sometimes, silence is enough. The washing ceremony was nearly complete. They dressed her in a white gown. And now, she looked like an angel.

A smiling angel.

Okasha had not moved since the moment his wife passed. He sat silent, folded into himself, his back still pressed against the door of Amara's room. The house was alive with whispers, but Okasha remained still.

Chad approached cautiously.

"Father, I have ordered the bowing of the Lune, and in a couple of hours, you will need to speak to the Orunians *at the Tribe's Home. We want to bury our mother today."*

Okasha did not respond. He did not blink.

Chad's jaw tightened.

"Father!"

No reaction.

Then, Okasha moved. His hand slipped into his pocket, fingers brushing against something. Slowly, he pulled out two envelopes and handed them to Chad.

"You or one of your brothers should read these letters to the people of Orun,*"* he said, voice low, distant. *"I will stay with your mother."*

Chad took the envelopes. He looked down at them, sealed. Concealed. His fingers tightened around the paper.

His father's voice remained calm. *"Do not open them until you reach the Tribe's Home."*

Word of Amara's death reached every corner of Orun. The leader of the Amázigh tribe could not believe it. He spoke to his daughter, Taziri, shaking his head in disbelief.

"I saw Amara *only one day before she passed. She was shining like a yellow rose."*

Taziri listened, but her mind was elsewhere. She was angry. But not at Nuro. At herself. She had been furious with him for not coming to their meeting. Now, she knew.

Now, she understood. She had been unjust to him. And he was nowhere to be seen.

By afternoon, Chad arrived. He stood in the center of the Tribe's Home, surrounded by hundreds of expectant eyes. In his hand, the two sealed envelopes.

He hesitated. Which one should he open first? Okasha hadn't told him. So, he made his choice. Both. He unfolded them and glanced at the signatures. One was signed Okasha Nogubane. The other, Amara. His mother. His breath caught. He began with hers.

Amara's Final Words

"Brothers and sisters,

What do I have to do with this world?

This world is a short journey, and I am a traveler who has returned to my new home.

Am I living?

*Yes. Inside my new home, gathered with the beloved brothers
and sisters who passed from your world into mine.*

I am happy now.

It is my destiny—one I saw within my Unabii.

Brothers and sisters, do not grieve for me.

I am at peace.

Until we meet again in my new home.

Your sister,

Amara."

Chad's eyes widened. As he finished reading, he leaned
back slightly, his forehead pulling away as if the words had
physically pushed him. He had known nothing about her Unabii.
She had kept it a secret. She had known she would die that day.
She had known she would be happy. And she had left them to
face her death unprepared.

Chad's fingers felt numb as he unfolded the second letter. His
father's handwriting was sharp. Clear. Final.

"I, King Okasha, *son of Nogubane,*

announce that my son, Nuro, son of Okasha,

is the Crown Prince of Orun.

This takes effect immediately.

Okasha *Nogubane.*"

Chad's mouth fell open slightly. His eyes stung as they ran over the words again. Then silence.

The weight of hundreds of eyes bore down on him.

The tribal leaders.

The people of Orun.

All watching. All waiting. This was humiliation. This was unbearable.

He hesitated.

Then, finally—he smiled.

But it was a stupid smile, one he instantly regretted—a smile that did not belong to him. His mother was dead, and he had smiled. He swallowed, hoping no one had seen it. Sweat trickled down his forehead. He wiped it away, scratching at the crease between his brows.

Then, he spoke.

> *"The burial ceremony will begin today at twin-sunfall from our home.*
>
> *Thank you."*

For the second time, Chad was not the chosen one. He could feel all of Orun watching, the tribal leaders, the people, and Taziri.

How do they see me now? Too small. Nothing.

His body shrank.

Smaller…Even smaller.

The crowd's eyes lowered, their necks stretching downward, searching for him.

Smaller.

Smaller.

Until he was so tiny that he vanished inside his own shoe.

It was dark inside. The air was warm with sweat and leather. He gasped for breath, his stomach twisting. He could not believe it. But it was happening before his eyes. The smell was suffocating. He had to get out.

"Hello! Hello!"

His voice echoed inside the shoe, bouncing back at him.

"Can anyone hear me?"

Nothing. Then, a sound.

Laughter. The crowd was laughing. They had heard him. And they were laughing.

For a moment, he felt good. No one could see him now. He had disappeared. His humiliation was erased.

But he could not stay here forever. He pressed his hands against the curved walls around him. A prison of his own making. He must leave. He pushed harder. His fingers met the rough, uneven stitching of the insole. The heat was unbearable, but he ignored it.

He climbed higher. There, he saw a sliver of light through the eyelet of his shoe, and then he crawled through it.

Fresh air. Cold.

Then, he finally sat on the shoelace, looking around. The audience was still laughing. But they couldn't see him. He was too tiny. They would step on him. Crush him. It was not safe outside. So, he jumped back in. Into the darkness. Then, a voice. Not laughter. Not an echo.

Warm.

Familiar.

"You are the greatest." "You are victorious."

The words repeated.

"You are the greatest." "You are victorious."

"You are the greatest." "You are victorious."

Each time, it grows louder.

"You are the greatest." "You are victorious."

The voice echoed, swelling with every repetition. Each word stretched through him, expanding, filling the space inside his mind, inside his very bones.

"You are the greatest." "You are victorious."

His body expanded with it.

Chad erupted like a volcano, surging upward, tearing through the sky. Now, he was the one who had to look down. To see those tiny ants, pathetic Orunians staring up in terror. He is the only voice that matters now. They could hear him. But he could no longer hear them. He could smash them. Crush them beneath his feet.

Then, the voice spoke again.

"You are eternal, my son."

His breath caught.

"Mother?"

"Yes, my son. I hear you. I feel you."

She had saved him from the darkness. She had lifted him up. And then, her final command.

"Kill Nuro, *my son. Kill him."*

Chad did not hesitate.

"I will do it, Mother."

The victorious Chad smiled. He is unstoppable now. But first, he would bury her.

Taziri, after watching Chad, felt a deeper worry settle inside her. Her thoughts drifted to Nuro. He was the Crown Prince now.

And she feared this would change him.

Would she lose him? Or had she already lost him?

The twin-sun fall of that never-ending day had arrived. Amara's four sons entered her room. She lay there, dressed in a white gown, her face still smiling, just as Nuro had left her. The room was full of colors, the air still carrying the scent of rosemary. They lifted the bier onto their shoulders, her body covered in a yellow cloth, her face uncovered.

They stepped outside the gate of Okasha's home. Beyond it, thousands of mourners waited. Nuro's chest tightened at the sight. He had hoped for a quiet, uncomplicated ceremony. But the crowd had gathered anyway.

The moment they opened the gate, the bier moved forward, slowly at first. On both sides, hundreds of Orunians waved palm branches, offering their final farewell to Amara.

Then, suddenly—the bier rushed forward like a bullet through the crowd.

Nuro's grip tightened.

"Slow down!" he called his brothers.

But they were already trying.

"It's not us," they said. *"We've slowed down. But the bier… it moves itself."*

Her sons were running after it. Nuro thought of what the washerwoman had said.

"It is her. It is her smell."

Now he knew—it was her.

Her bier was carrying itself forward, rushing toward its final resting place. Maybe she wanted to meet her husband, who was already waiting for her inside the grave. Perhaps she wanted to see her new home, the one she had dreamed of.

They reached the Okasha family tomb. The mourners stopped outside. Only the tribal leaders, the Siddiq, and her four sons followed the bier through the gate. As she passed through, Amara felt something.

She was not alone.

The six souls of Okasha's family stood there, waiting for her. They were smiling.

Amara was not afraid. She had been preparing for this moment all along.

At the final place, they reached her grave. Okasha was already inside. Standing in the hole he had dug only a few days ago, a grave he had once prepared for himself. But now, he realized, he had been digging it for her. He remembered it. The feeling of clawing at the dirt, like a desperate animal, digging, digging, and digging. And yet, she was stronger than him. She had pulled him out of that hole. She had kept her secret, her Unabii, her death, hidden from him.

Okasha felt weak. For the first time in his life, he felt helpless. Tears poured into the grave, dripping onto the dirt like a broken tap that could not be shut off.

The bier was lowered into the grave. Okasha received her body, laid her gently over the earth, then reached out, wrapping his right hand around her neck, then he leaned in, bringing his lips close to her ear, whispering something only the soil would hear. His sons did not hear it. They did not understand. But Amara heard. And she smiled. He had told her:

"Wait for me in our new home."

Then, Okasha kissed her.

First, her eyes.

Then, her nose.

Then, just before giving her the final kiss on her forehead, he collapsed onto her chest. Like a child clinging to his mother. He stayed there. Long enough for Nuro to finally whisper:

"Father."

But neither Nuro nor his brothers knew what to do. None of them could pull their father away. Until the leader of the Amazigh tribe climbed down into the grave.

He placed a firm hand on Okasha's shoulder.

"It's time to go now." And he pulled him out of the grave.

The soil began to fall.

This was it.

A small hole... Beneath the dirt...

Okasha's mind drifted to Siddiq's words.

Destiny of the Creator is like an arrow, shot behind you from the moment of your birth.

Run, run, like a beast...

Run, run, run...

Salt and Heart

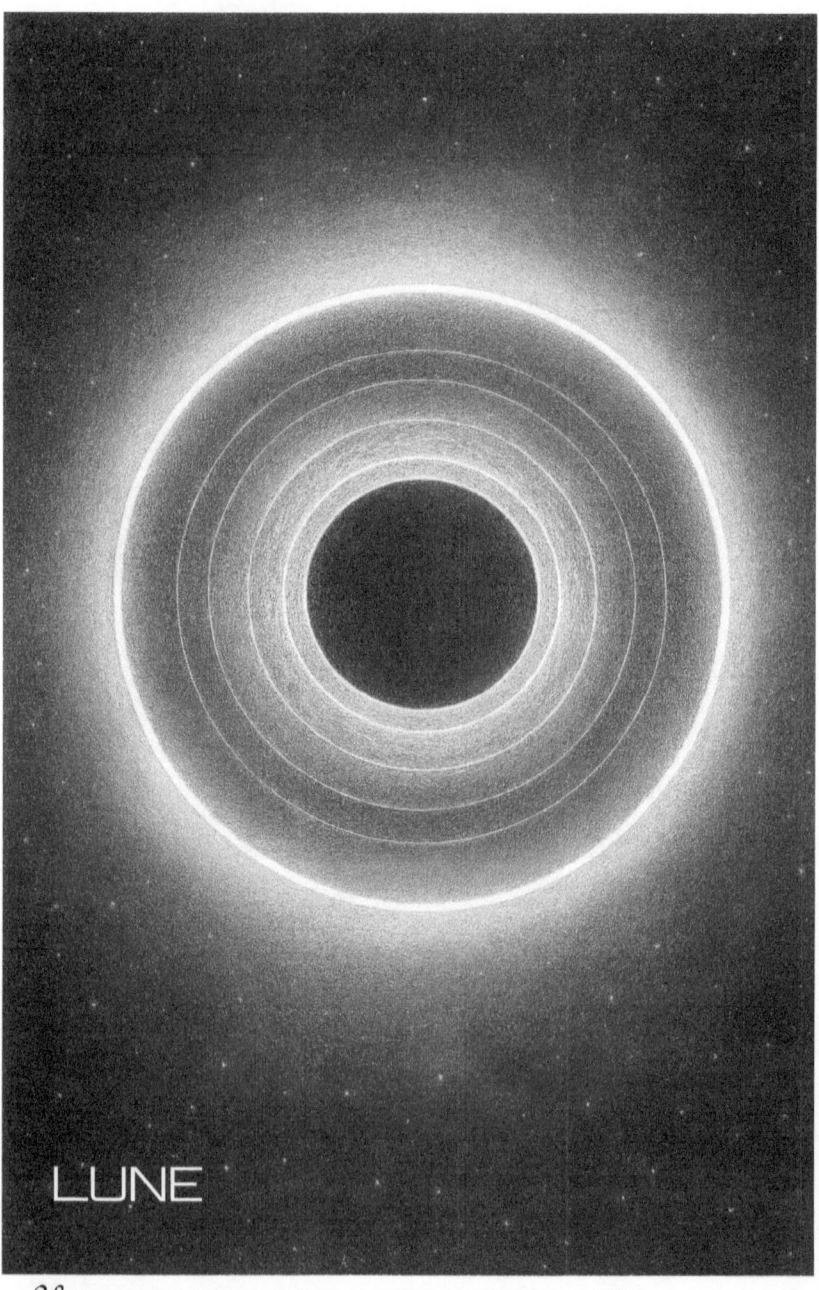

LUNE

She searched for him everywhere. She tried to find him, to speak to him, to tell him what she was feeling, but he had vanished.

Taziri had changed.

She was no longer the girl she used to recognize in the mirror. She had lost weight. Her appetite had disappeared. Her stomach always felt full, though she barely ate. She only drank enough to keep herself alive. Her mind circled one thought. The same thought that erupted the moment she opened her eyes. The same thought that echoed when she closed them. The same thought with every breath.

Taziri was exhausted.

Every time she overcame one battle, another rose to take its place. But this one—this one was the worst. It wasn't just heart versus mind anymore. It was mind against itself. Hemisphere against hemisphere. Dignity against addiction.

Her heart was wounded.

It hurt in a real, physical way, like a stabbing knife slipping between her ribs, pressing inward. She felt it with every breath. Even when she held her breath, the pain didn't ease. It just stayed.

Sometimes she imagined her own heart presiding like a judge, but its verdict was always the same: her heart belonged to him. And her eyes—the only witnesses—gave the same testimony. They, too, belonged to him.

But eventually, she made a quiet decision.

A private settlement—she would stop chasing him. She would protect what little dignity she had left. Still… she would visit that Place, her hidden Heaven, where he might have been, where they both used to be, because even a memory could soothe the ache, the withdrawal.

Suddenly, Professor Casablanca stopped, as if something had forced him into silence. The waves were rising, crashing harder and harder against the Panthalassic wall. The atmosphere, so calm just moments ago, had changed.

It now felt unfamiliar. Even the scent of the ocean had shifted from salty breeze to something else—something like the scent of soup… or wet foam. The twin suns disappeared behind thick clouds. Darkness fell. The golden rays are gone.

Still, the professor said nothing. His silence lingered. Then he turned his head slowly to the right. And stared, as if a ghost were standing there.

The waves grew even higher. There was no wind. No moon. Only wave upon wave, leaping over one another, growing larger with each crash.

I felt it then, rage.

Not mine, not his.

The rage came from the ocean as if the waves were trying to speak. As if something was trapped beneath them, deep in the water, struggling to be heard. Then, Professor Casablanca pointed at me. I waited. I thought he was going to ask me something.

But instead, he continued…

Our human history does not march forward; it loops, spirals, and echoes. Since the first civilizations, humankind has been trapped in a relentless cycle of wars, betrayals, rises, and downfalls. Again and again, the past remakes itself, repeating like the echo of voices across time—almost the same voice, speaking in different ages. The same stories unfold, often in the same places, with only the characters' names changed, mocking those who believe they can escape it.

Thirty-four years ago, I stood at the threshold of manhood, Roy—still shadowed by the boy I used to be. I was the one sitting in the last row of the classroom circle. My teachers thought I was lazy, always hiding back there in the shadows. But I had my reasons. It wasn't laziness. The year Amara *died…That year, Homowo Day was different. It wasn't like the other years. There was no celebration. It was supposed to be an ordinary day. But everything turned upside down.*

That day, Taziri decided to return to the place where it all began, the hidden plain between the two mountains above Orun's lake. Where she had once waited for him… and he never came.

She prepared everything just as before. She laid out her mat. She gathered slices of sweet yellow mango—his favorite—and poured fresh mango juice into a small container. It was exactly the same. She smiled as she prepared it all, imagining the perfect romantic reunion under the light of the *Lune.*

She imagined herself watching him—watching him long for the mango juice—watching him enjoy each slice. That look on his face—the one he always had when tasting the mangos he loved—would be enough for her now. More than enough. She packed everything with quiet passion and rode her horse up the hill.

And then, she caught a scent. Something warm. Pleasant. A woody fragrance that reminded her of him.

She smiled. The stabbing pain between her ribs began to soften. She could breathe again. Her heartbeat quickened as she climbed higher.

Then, she saw him. Up there. Waiting.

In that moment, her mind surrendered. No more voices. No more dignity. No more pain. The knife inside her chest disappeared.

And something strange stirred in her stomach—Hunger.

Real hunger. Something she hadn't felt in days. She had found it. The cure. The medication for her withdrawal.

But when she reached the top... he wasn't there.

No one was.

Nuro had only been in her mind. Her craving had turned into delirium.

The scent. The smile. His longing gaze at the mangoes—All of it, only inside her head.

Taziri sat down, spread out the mat, and gently placed the mangoes and juice before her. She waited. But waiting—She couldn't bear it anymore.

And yet...

There was peace inside her. A strange peace, earned after her last internal settlement: Not to run after him. To let it happen, if it ever did, on its own. Then, A thought erupted....

What if I kept searching? What if I went back down and looked for him again?

The beating of war drums had started once more. That thought did not comply with her treaty. Not with the fragile dignity she had just reclaimed. So, Taziri let it pass. She didn't move. She stayed. And stared at the *Lune* above.

At that same hour, Chad was preparing himself for something great, greater than Homowo Day itself. He wore a black Asiago military suit. It looked more suited for war than celebration, not that there was a celebration this year; Homowo had been canceled. He stood in front of the mirror, inspecting himself. His posture was perfect, and his chin was proud.

But something was missing. It should have been there, right where he left it—A year ago, after his great victory. He turned to the bed and bent down. There it was.

His sword.

Still in its place. Exactly where he'd left it, he picked it up and grasped it with both hands. The blade was corroded with dried blood from the last war. He hadn't cleaned it.

Why would he?

Something fresher would soon replace that blood. Something warmer. He turned again to the mirror. Now... now the missing part had returned. He stood tall, complete, swelling with pride. Then, slowly, he moved toward the window on his right.

He opened it, and with a single strike from the base of his sword, he shattered the glass from the outside. The shards flew inward, raining across the room, scattering across the floor beneath his feet, just as he intended. Then he raised the sword and stabbed at the ceiling. Once. Twice. A third time, the blade lowered. Point down. Tip grazing the floor.

And again, he stared into the mirror. He waited. And waited. Waiting for something great.

For a wave.

For a visitor.

For Roy, the younger version of Professor Casablanca, it was his first *Homowo* Day in Orun without a celebration. At first, it seemed like any ordinary day. He was excited. Curious about the origin of *Homowo*, a story that had come from the Ga people—a celebration born from famine. But he was even more curious about Zangbeto, these strange spinning straw structures—night watchers that guarded the streets in old legends.

Roy continued:

"I used to sit in the last row of the classroom. I liked keeping the Lune in view, framed in the sky through the high windows. I felt attached to her, especially after leaving Barzakh. She gave me a sense of safety.

Our teacher began writing on the chalkboard. His hands were darker than the board itself. I loved that sound—the chalk dragging across the surface, the powder falling like snowflakes to the floor. He wrote only two words:

Ga *on the right.*

Agun *on the left.*

It was the perfect beginning, the perfect story to tell.

But he didn't brush the chalk from his hands when he finished writing. He didn't even clap them clean. He turned around, his hands still coated in white dust, and began to speak. Not about Homowo. Not about Zangbeto. He talked about

Amara. *He said he could never forget two things about her: her smile and her scent. And just then, we heard something."*

It started faint—a tremor in the air. Barely audible at first, then growing louder. It stretched, warped, and cracked, until it became a scream. A man's voice, distorted through some broken speaker. Agonizing. Raw. Inside the classroom, they all looked at each other.

What was that sound? Who was screaming? Why wouldn't it stop?

The sound filled everything. It shook the glass in the windows, vibrated in the walls, crawled into our skulls, and pierced our ears like a blade.

The teacher waited. He heard it too. He opened his mouth and said something, but no one could hear him. The scream was too loud. Then he shouted:

"It's a siren. A warning. Stay calm! It might just be a training."

That was the last thing Roy remembered before darkness took him. He opened his eyes. Dust was everywhere. Thick in the air. Floating in streaks of dim light.

He couldn't see his hands. The screaming had stopped, but now there was nothing. Only pressure, something heavy pressing against his eardrums. He was lying on his back. He lifted his head slowly and looked at his hands. They were covered in chalk powder. Nothing looked familiar. Nothing felt right.

Was I unconscious? Did I black out?

He looked down and tried to move his legs.

No response, Panic flared.

Am I paralyzed?

But no, he could feel sensation. Just not movement. Then he realized—those weren't his feet. They belonged to a classmate, collapsed across his legs.

As his vision cleared, he saw the room in fragments: Bodies in a tangled pile—his classmates, gathered in one corner like toys in a basket.

He stood, slowly. Some of them were bleeding. All of them could walk, but like ghosts, like children playing blind man's buff.

He stepped forward. Glass cracked underfoot. Their teacher was slumped against the door, blood running down his face like a silent shower. His lips were moving, but Roy couldn't hear a word. Then the teacher walked out. A few students followed.

But Roy stayed behind. He wanted to see her. *The Lune.* He always felt safe with her. She was his anchor. He walked toward the window. The dust was settling. As he neared the frame, the other students suddenly ran.

They screamed and scattered. Roy turned back to the window and saw something dark hanging just outside. The shape was unclear: a form, a weight, something suspended from the frame.

He took a step closer.

A thief? Climbing into our classroom? I have to run like the others.

But his legs didn't move. His brain gave the order—Nothing. His body was rigid. Rigor mortis of fear. His hands trembled, but his eyes locked on the figure at the window. Watching its next move. He stood there, facing it, facing his destiny alone.

Just moments before, Taziri had been lost in thought, staring at the *Lune*. Still. Silent. Waiting.

In a single flicker of her eyelid, the light vanished. The lunar ring were gone, swallowed by sudden darkness.

In the next blink—a blinding halo of fire erupted in the sky. It pulsed outward like a living thing, expanding, devouring the void.

Then came the storm. Burning fragments rained down over Orun, like fire hail crashing from the sky. She didn't have time to scream. The shockwave hit. It threw her to the ground.

Her mat, her juice, the mango slices all lifted, scattered, lost in the wind. She lay flat, her breath knocked out of her. Something crushed her chest, pressing her heart with invisible force, squeezing it.

When she woke from the fall, there was only one thought—

Him, Nuro.

She had to go down, find him, and protect him from the fire falling from the sky. She would give her life for him. She didn't look back; she left the mangoes, left the juice. With a single, fierce motion, she swung herself over her horse, like a thunderbolt unleashed. And she rode down through the flames to find the missing.

Before the explosion wave reached Chad's room, he stood motionless in front of the mirror. The siren blared outside—but to him, it was music.

Calming. Sacred.

He didn't flinch, not even when the *Lune* exploded or the sky lit up with fire.

He waited for the wave to arrive. When it came crashing through the shattered window, he didn't move even one inch. He stood still, leaning on his sword. His victorious sword.

Then, the visitor arrived.

The voice...

"My son...

You have risen again today.

You are pure.

You are incomparable.

Look"

Chad turned slowly to the window. Outside—the sky burned. Fireworks erupted within the smoke. The *Lune* had fallen. His eyes gleamed.

"Look…The toxic placenta has fallen.

The sky is suffering."

He saw it—perfect. The sky wept tears of flame. Orunians ran like ants, scattering from their crushed colony. No more shelters. No more refuge. Orun was kneeling. Beneath his will. Under his dominion.

But something still felt… missing. He could feel it—a gap in the moment, an empty note in the symphony.

Then the voice returned:

"Son, I'm proud.

I am so proud of my pure son.

But we still need more."

Chad nodded, eyes fixed on the fire falling from the sky.

"Take your present," the voice said.

"Remember the last one—the sword, the victorious?"

Chad looked around.

"It's in your pocket.

The pocket of your suit."

His breath quickened. He slid his hand inside the pocket and felt something sharp and hard. He drew it out slowly, and his face lit up, radiant, like an angel of death.

The *"present"* in his hands: *Two stingray barbs, taken from the tails of dead Stingrays.*

> ***"You've earned the highest rank,"*** the voice whispered.

> ***"Place them on your epaulettes, where they belong."***

Chad obeyed. He pinned the barbs on each shoulder, one by one.

Pure Chad *is reborn...*

The placenta has fallen...

Roy stood rooted in place, his hand trembling as he watched, waiting for the thief's next move. He didn't blink; he kept his eyes locked on the figure hanging halfway through the window.

But nothing happened. The man didn't move. He just hung there, his upper body slumped inside the classroom, arms stretched, hands grazing the floor. His lower half was still outside. His face was pressed against the wall, and his long hair fell like a curtain, almost touching the ground.

Roy's mind was racing.

A thief? But what would a thief want from a classroom in chaos—chalk?

Slowly, the stiffness in Roy's legs began to melt. The rigor of fear relaxed. He stepped closer. The ground beneath him was sticky. He looked down. He was standing in a pool of blood.

Fresh. Dark.
Still growing. It was all coming from the hanging man. From his arms. From his head. From his entire body.

Roy stared, certain now—*he's dead.*

But then, the man's chest moved.

Inhale.

Roy's breath caught.

He's alive.

And now Roy couldn't leave.

He couldn't run. He had to help. He moved closer. Closer. Until he stood directly in front of him.

Then he froze again.

That long "hair" brushing the ground, what he had seen earlier—the curtain—wasn't hair at all. It was a scalp, torn from the skull, now lying on the ground like a peeled eggshell. The white of his skull was exposed.

Roy bent down. Gently, with shaking hands, he picked up the scalp and placed it back over the man's skull. A useless gesture. But a human one.

He tried to recognize the man. But there were no features left to recognize. The face was swollen and blue, strangled, covered in blood. The nose had been crushed, twisted to one side.

Roy's stomach clenched. He stepped back. The broken glass cracked under his feet, crunching softly, blood-soaked.

Then, he saw it—a large shard of glass protruding from the man's back. Roy circled him. It wasn't just on his back. It had entered through the front—his stomach—and passed all the way through. Roy reached to remove it, but the man moaned, a sound full of pain and exhaustion. Roy's thoughts scattered and vanished. He couldn't pull it out. It would kill him.

And then, A whisper. It was so faint that he almost couldn't hear it.

"Water... water..."

Without thinking, Roy turned and ran. He had to bring him water.

At the exact moment Taziri rode down toward the city, she saw dragons circling above Orun, dozens of them, sweeping through the sky like vultures over a battlefield.

Smoke coiled upward, thick and unrelenting. The city was no longer the city she knew. It looked like something rotten, like flies swarming over the swollen carcass of a dead animal—one that had died long ago. Its stench was so heavy that it seemed to take shape in the air.

The air of Orun was suffocating, choked with ash. There was no escape from it. Taziri pulled her scarf up, covering her nose and mouth. As she entered the city, she saw thousands of Orunians heading toward the tribe's home. Many of them were limping. Bleeding. The fire fragments had stopped falling, but the damage was done.

No one knew what had truly happened. Only one truth lingered in the air:

The *Lune* was down. Some whispered it was a WAOFO attack; others said nothing, eyes wide, still in shock.

Taziri searched among the crowds. Faces blurred past her, panicked, injured, confused. But he wasn't there. Still, she went with them, moving toward the tribe's home. Maybe he'll be there…. The missing.

Thousands of Orunians had gathered, filling every space inside and outside the Tribe's home. It felt like the day of resurrection. Taziri entered, eyes scanning the crowd, searching for him. She couldn't see him. Only strangers, but she kept searching.

Then, she saw her father. She slipped behind him, heart pounding faster than a rainstorm.

Then Chad appeared.

Flanked by his loyal Ray Riders, he stepped forward. Behind him came Okasha, his father.

The old man looked frail, broken by grief, as if the sudden loss of Amara had drained the last of his strength. Kato and Fahd supported him, guiding him to sit behind Chad.

But still—Where is Nuro?

Taziri's neck stretched like a mongoose, eyes darting across the crowd.

But he wasn't there. That was what she feared most. The whole family was here, except him. Something has happened to him. The thought wrapped around her ribs like a fist. Her knees weakened. Her breath grew short.

Something happened.

Okasha looks like a man already in mourning.

Chad... Chad is about to announce it.

Taziri couldn't bear to wait. Dragging her heavy limbs, she pushed through the crowd toward Kato.

But just as she reached him—Chad began to speak in a steady, strong voice:

"O Orunians,"

"I am the guardian of Orun's Heaven.

I hold two keys."

"The Key of Heaven"

He raised his left hand.

"I close its doors. No one may cross again."

"And the Key of Eternal Hell"

He lifted the other hand.

I will open its seven doors.

Hell craves. It hungers.

It waits for those with angel faces and Satan's hearts.

The fire will sear their skin."

Taziri stared at Chad, stunned. She looked at her father beside her, searching his face for clarity, but he looked just as confused. None of it made sense. Chad wasn't even looking at them as he spoke; his eyes were elsewhere, wild, lost in another realm.

Then Fahd stepped forward and tried to interrupt. He said, loud and steady.

*"It was a **WAOFO** attack; they did it. They launched missiles from our own land... and they took down the Lune."*

He looked out over the crowds.

"The WAOFOs are among us now."

Pause.

We've made a decision, and we ask for your pledge."

But Chad shoved his brother aside with his shoulder, voice rising again:

*"The Panthalassic wall will be permanently closed.
The crossers among us—the traitors—will be deported. There will be no more food chains reaching Barzakh..."*

A gasp slipped from Taziri's lips.

"Orunians!" Chad bellowed.

"There is only one refuge—through me!

Daima Orun! Daima Orun!"

He raised both arms high as if to bless or curse them. Taziri couldn't stay silent any longer. She stepped forward, her voice sharp, cutting through the noise:

"No departure!

You have no authority to make this decision!

Where is the king? Where is our Crown Prince?"

The crowd stirred. Chad's Ray Riders moved quickly. They came down toward her, seized her by the arms, and began dragging her out of the Tribe's home. On her way out, she saw Kato.

She struggled against the guards, reached out to him, and gasped:

"Where is Nuro?"

Kato met her eyes. His voice was quiet, heavy. *"He's with his mother."*

Her stomach dropped. The world tilted. The weight returned—heavier than before. It pulled her down like gravity itself. She collapsed to her knees.

"He's gone," she whispered, her voice faint and broken.

Buried beneath the dirt beside Amara.

Then, Kato noticed her shock. He knelt beside her, his voice soft, urgent:

"Taziri… He still lives. He's only visiting her."

It took her a second to register the words. And then, life rushed back into her limbs. The crushing weight lifted. She stood instantly. *"He's not dead…?"* she said, breathless.

"Dead? Taziri, *what's wrong with you?"* Kato asked, bewildered.

She didn't answer. She pushed the Ray Riders away with surprising strength and ran.

Ran like a wild rabbit.

No horse. No farewell to her father. Just her feet pounding the ground. Toward Amara's grave.

Around Amara's grave, seven souls stood silently. Amara's soul was among them. They watched as salty tears fell—one after another—onto the soil of her Grave. They came from Nuro. Her son. In all the days since her death, he had resisted the truth that she was gone. He had been silent. Not broken, just empty.

He hadn't cried.

He hadn't mourned.

He felt nothing.

He had worn a heart of stone.

But now, today, that stone heart had shattered into dust. Now, finally, he realized that she was gone. Only today did he feel the emptiness she left behind. He was standing in front of her grave, thinking of her last words:

"We are all one. From one."

He had questions, so many questions. Her mysterious death. The radiation in her body. Where had it come from? Barzakh?

Was that why she visited Siddiq? *He must know something.*

Then, Nuro felt it. Someone was behind him. He didn't turn. He didn't need to. He knew the scent.

Taziri.

Her presence warmed the air. But he didn't turn to her, he couldn't. He was crying, and she could not see him like this.

Quietly, he swept his fallen tears from the earth over Amara's grave with his foot, hiding the evidence of his grief.

Taziri waited. She didn't speak at first. She didn't want to invade his silence. But she could only hold it for a few seconds. Then, softly, a whisper:

> "Nuro... *I'm sorry for your loss.*
> *I searched for you everywhere.*
> *I was suffering.*
> *And I... I need to tell you something."*

She paused. Her thoughts tangled. Maybe now wasn't the right time. Maybe she should wait to confess how she felt. But waiting had no place anymore in Taziri's life. She stepped closer.

> *"Can you please look at me?"*

He didn't move. The tears had stopped, but he kept his back to her.

> "Nuro, *look into my eyes.*
> *I'm not talking to myself.*
> *We need you.*
> *You are our Crown Prince.*
> *Your brother... your brother wants to deport the crossers.*
> *And I won't allow him to.*
> *Not over my body."*

Silence. Still nothing.

> *"Nuro... are you with me?"*

But he wasn't. He was somewhere else. Inside his grief. Inside that private world that had cracked open today, finally letting his sorrow pour out.

Taziri's eyes widened, veins bulging. She clenched her jaw. Her voice broke.

> "Nuro, *it's disrespectful.*
> *Not even a word? Not even a glance?*
> *I searched for you. I thought about you.*
> *I don't deserve this.*
> *Why are you treating me like this?"*

Her heart broke, and then, she cried, tears she had held back for days.

> "Nuro... *say anything.*
> *Anything.*
> *It's serious now."*

Nothing. Not a word.

Then, with sharpness, Taziri exploded: *"Be a man!"*

Silence. A pause. A breath.

And then she spoke again, quieter now, her voice trembling:

> *"I'll go,* Nuro.
> *I'll go.*
> *Forever."*

She turned. Walked away. Didn't look back. Left him there, alone with the grave, alone with the silence.

Also, Roy left that hanging man alone with his suffering. He ran down the stairs, across the courtyard of his school, toward the water dispenser. He didn't even look up at the missing *Lune*.

His hands were shaking. He couldn't even fill the glass halfway. There was no time to calm down. No breath to catch. He held his right hand with his left, trying to steady the tremor. Finally, the glass was full.

He turned and saw them. Two Ray Riders are standing in the distance, outside the gate of his school. He waved, shouted:

"Help! Help!"

They ran toward him. Relief surged in Roy's chest.

Finally, help is coming.

Inside the classroom, the hanging man waited. Thirst, that was all he felt. No pain anymore. Just the dull hum of nothingness.

He could no longer feel his legs. His brain sent commands, but there was no response. His head tingled with numbness. His hope for Roy's return had dimmed. He feared that Roy would leave, like all the others.

The Ray Riders reached Roy. No questions. No warning. They slammed him to the ground—glass of water shattering in his hand. Grabbed him by the back of his shirt and yanked him upright.

Roy gasped:

"There's a man inside, injured.
He needs water.
Please, he's dying."

One of the Riders asked, ***"What's his name?"***

Roy forgot how to breathe. He didn't know. But his mouth answered:

"Mr. Paul."

The Riders exchanged a glance. They said nothing. Then they tied Roy's hands behind his back, shoved him down onto his face, and dragged him away.

Mr. Paul had been right to doubt. Roy didn't return.

Inside the shattered classroom, the man's numbness crept upward, past his spine, into his neck.

His arms—paralyzed.

His body—unmoving.

Only his chest rose and fell. Only his eyelids could blink. He saw the world now through a hazy red. His thirst deepened.

His wish was simple:

Just one drop.
Just one drop of water before I die.

His throat was dry, coated with salt he couldn't swallow. Too weak to even gulp his own saliva. His heart slowed. There wasn't much blood left to pump—just a thin trickle, like air leaking from a punctured bladder.

He began to feel something sharp—tiny salt crystals, scratching inside his throat.

His heart stopped. No more blood. It was empty.

The punctured bladder collapsed.

His throat closed. Air couldn't pass through.

Choked by dryness. By salt.

Last Standing Tooth

UNABII

Nuro saw his brother Chad, unusually cheerful, standing before an enormous curtain that stretched across the entire horizon. Chad wore a black Asiago suit, with two small, dead stingrays resting on each shoulder. He looked no older than fifteen. In his hand, he held a bubble wand toy.

As Nuro approached, he asked, *"What are you doing?"*

Chad didn't answer. He didn't even look at him. Didn't seem to hear.

As Nuro approached, an offensive, rotting stench filled the air. The toy—meant for bubbles—was releasing not air but rotten eggs. The eggs spilled out slowly, slithering toward the curtain.

Nuro moved the curtain aside. The smell grew worse. Behind it was a vast blue desert and a large, gaping hole in the center. Around the hole stood hundreds of people... without heads.

They stood balanced on the tips of spears. He heard the name echo through the Unabii:

The Spearhead Clan

They surrounded the hole, dumping rotten eggs into it. Each egg disappeared into the darkness below.

Suddenly, screams filled the air—from the sky, from the ground, and from between the particles of the blue sand. It was the kind of screaming that made the ground tremble and the sand ripple—as if the earth itself was caught in an earthquake of grief.

Then, he saw them.

Thousands upon thousands of people—suffering. They slid across the sand, packed onto two small plates, pushed forward by the Spearhead Clan toward the hole.

The suffering people had no hearts, only empty chests.

Their bodies wept, cried, and screamed as they slid forward. They begged for help, but no one helped. As they reached the hole, they stepped onto the rotten eggs.

The eggs cracked beneath them.

One after another—They fell.

They vanished.

The blue desert swallowed them like quicksand.

And then Nuro felt it, a coldness, deeper than winter, piercing through his bones, into his teeth as if his bones had turned to cold metal.

He turned back toward Chad, still behind the curtain.

Chad was still smiling.

#

Nuro woke with a jolt. It was warm inside his room, but he felt cold. His teeth ached with a strange pain. He knew what this was.

It wasn't just a dream. It was Unabii.

And it wasn't the first time. It was the third night in a row. The same vision. The same screams. Still echoing inside his ears. He sat on the edge of his bed and began to write it down with each detail clear in his mind.

The headless clan. The rotten eggs. The hole. The heartless people.

He stared at the words.

What does it mean?

Why didn't I help them?

Even if it was an illusion, he felt guilty. They had needed him, and he did nothing. Just then, Kato walked in. He noticed Nuro's pale face, his heavy breath.

"Son of my mother," Kato said, half-joking.

"Did you come back from the dead this morning?"

Nuro glanced at him. His voice was quiet:

"Better to stay among the dead...

I'm not ready. It's too heavy for me.

I wasn't ready for this. The crown, the responsibility... I just started my life."

He paused. Then added,

"And I feel a distance between me and my brothers.

Fahd... Chad... *I understand them.*

And I'm seriously thinking of giving it back."

Kato blinked. *"What do you mean?"*

"The position. The title. The Crown Prince. It doesn't feel like mine."

Silence fell between them. Then Kato spoke again, softer now:

"Nuro... *not now. Brother, this isn't the time to take that step.*

But tell me...have you seen her?"

Nuro looked up. *"Who?"*

"Our mother... I see her almost every day now. Did you dream of her?"

Nuro shook his head.

"No. Not yet.

But I feel it, this emptiness.

Endless emptiness.

She left behind a space that nothing can fill."

Kato nodded slowly. Then added:

"Before I forget... did you see Taziri?

I saw her recently. She looked... destroyed.

Heartbroken."

But before Kato could finish the sentence—Nuro stood. Quietly pulled on his clothes. Kato raised an eyebrow.

"Where are you going?"

Nuro smiled faintly. *"I have to do something."*

Kato smirked.

"Wow. That took two seconds. Fastest transformation I've ever seen."

Nuro slipped out the door. Kato sank into Nuro's bed, finally letting his body rest after their short conversation.

In front of her home, Taziri called out:

"Leith! Leith!"

Her horse stood at a distance, far from the gate, grazing greedily on thick grass.

She called again. "Leith!"

Still, no reaction. He didn't even lift his head. Not a flick of the ear. Not a glance in her direction.

Taziri frowned, tension rising.

"That's enough! Your belly's going to explode!"

She started walking toward him, frustration mixing with guilt.

"Leith …"

Still nothing. Not even a swish of his tail. She approached him more and gently laid her hand on his back. His skin twitched beneath her touch, but he kept chewing, ignoring her entirely.

"Hey," she whispered.

"Come on… I know. I left to see Nuro *without saying goodbye. I'm sorry. I shouldn't have done that. Not without you."*

She moved closer, aiming to hug him around the neck. But he turned away, deliberately, giving her his back, still chewing like a beast.

Taziri sighed. "Leith, *man!*"

She ran around to the other side, reaching for him again. But he turned away, again.

"*Stop acting like a baby!*" she muttered.

Then, she had an idea.
She drifted toward his side, pretending to reach for his neck. She paused. Waited.

And just when he turned to avoid her—She spun around and darted the other way, throwing her arms around his neck.

She held him tightly. "*Now you can't escape!*"

But he did. With a stubborn toss, he pulled his neck free.

Taziri held her hands on her hips, exasperated.

"Leith ... *you didn't need to be jealous.*"

She softened.

"*You know I'll never leave you. You are my first deepest love.*"

She smiled, and for the first time, his ears flicked forward. His skin relaxed. She approached again, hopeful, but again, he turned away.

"*Fine,*" she said with a shrug.

"*Have it your way.*"

She turned and began walking back toward the door of her home. But before she could reach it, Leith darted ahead and blocked the door with his body.

Taziri laughed.

"Leith ... *what now?*"

She tried to lead him aside, but he ran ahead again and blocked the door a second time.

He was enjoying this. Teasing her. Playing with her.

Taziri shook her head.

"*You little devil,*" she smiled.

"*I'm not even going to ride you. I just need to rest.*"

Her voice softened.

"*I missed you more than I thought.*"

Then, he began to lick her face. She giggled, trying to push him away.

"*Hey! Enough!* Leith, *stop!*"

She laughed. Finally, she hugged him. And this time, he let her. Then, slowly, he stepped aside.

Only then did she open the door and step inside.

"*You playful baby Panda,*" she whispered, grinning.

Taziri finally stepped inside her home. She closed the door behind her, leaned her back against it, and exhaled deeply. A small, uncontainable smile tugged at her lips. She thought of him.

But she shook her head—*I must distract myself.* She moved toward the kitchen.

The first thing she saw was the mangoes piled neatly in the fruit basket, their sweet citrus scent filling the room.

She smiled again.

He is everywhere, even in the air.

Knock. Knock.

The door.

She hurried back, opened it, and found herself face-to-face with him…. Leith.

She burst out laughing.

"What are you doing here?"

Then a voice spoke from behind Leith:

"It's me, Nuro."

Taziri laughed even harder.

"You can talk, Leith? *I didn't know you had it in you."*

Nuro's voice came again, slightly muffled.

"Hey, I'm not your horse! I'm behind him! And he's not letting me through. I'm afraid he'll kick me."

Taziri chuckled, reaching out to stroke Leith's face.

"It's all right. He's a friend. We'll let him in, just this once."

She kissed Leith on the forehead and smiled at Nuro. Finally, Leith stepped aside, but he kept a close eye on Nuro.

Without a word, Taziri threw her arms around Nuro. She said nothing. Just smiled against him, breathing in his scent. It felt like breathing again after being underwater. After a moment, Nuro spoke:

"I think he doesn't like me.

I swear he's planning to bite me."

As if on cue, Leith turned his head sharply toward Nuro. Taziri kept clinging to him, laughing softly.

Then Nuro asked:

"Taziri... *may I come inside?"*

She didn't answer. Her arms still around his neck, Nuro simply stepped forward, carrying her gently into the house.

Behind them, Leith snorted loudly.

"You hear that?" Nuro said, grinning.

Taziri just smiled wider. Suddenly, a voice called from upstairs:

"Taziri*! Who's there?"*

Taziri immediately jumped off Nuro and pushed him away lightly. She called back:

"It's Leith!"

Then, smiling mischievously, she placed a hand on Nuro's shoulder. Nuro muttered under his breath:

"*Not again...*"

Then louder:

"*It's me.* Nuro*!*"

Her father's voice came again:

"*Wait! I'll come down.*"

Taziri could have stayed in Nuro's arms forever, just that moment had made her life feel full again. Her father descended the stairs, greeting Nuro warmly. Meanwhile, Taziri slipped away to prepare Nuro's favorite mango slices and juice. As she moved through the kitchen, she heard them speaking.

Her father's voice grew serious:

"*We must prevent this massacre,* Nuro.

What your brother is planning, we cannot allow it.

The land is enough for all of us.

No departures. No separations.

Are you with us?"

Nuro nodded solemnly.

"*Of course. But it won't be easy.*

Chad *has twisted the fall of the Lune to serve himself.*

And those Ray Riders—they're his slaves.

They don't think. They obey.

If Chad commands it, they'll carry it out.

And with those elite soldiers at his side, Chad is the most powerful man in Orun."

Her father frowned but stayed calm.

"Still, we have one chance.

At the harbor.

We can block the departure."

Taziri reentered the room, carrying the plate of mango slices. Her father continued:

"Tomorrow, we'll gather at the harbor.

Some tribal leaders will join us. Even the Siddiq.

Together, we'll stand like a wall."

The whole time, Taziri's eyes never left Nuro. She was flying inside, full of light.

Then Nuro asked, thoughtfully:

"Who are the WAOFO?"

Her father answered:

"We don't know. They work in the shadows. Sometimes they leave behind a trace, a symbol, a sentence. I saw one once, written on the Panthalassic wall beside their mark: 'We are one from one."

Nuro was silent. He had heard those words before on his mother's deathbed. The room seemed to tilt for a moment, but he caught himself.

Taziri's father smiled gently:

> *"Tomorrow. At the harbor. We'll stand together."*

He rose, extending his hand to Nuro before leaving. Nuro shook it.

> *"Till tomorrow, then,* Nuro."

But Nuro lingered. He stood like a statue, completely still.

Her father looked puzzled. *"Is there something else?"*

Nuro smiled sheepishly.

"I want to leave...but there's a problem."

He tilted his head toward the door.

"Leith *is blocking the way."*

Her father chuckled.

> *"Ah, that's it*! Taziri, *help our guest."*

Laughing, Taziri led Leith away. Before Nuro stepped out, Taziri leaned close to him and whispered:

> *"See you tomorrow...you brownie bear."*

Then she turned and ran inside, laughing.

Outside, Nuro stood there, stunned. *"Brownie bear? Bear?"*

He shook his head, laughing. But as he walked away, Leith fixed him with a hard stare. Nuro immediately tensed up and hurried off.

The two Ray Riders who had tied Roy at school dragged him through the streets. When they reached the crowd, they untied his hands and shoved him forward.

Roy stumbled.

Before him stretched a river of people, thousands moving in one direction, herded like animals between walls of armed Ray Riders on either side, watching, silent, unmoving. Roy was pushed into the moving mass. He looked around, through the crowds, confused.

Why were they all so sad? Why were they carrying bundles over their heads, blankets, pots, and clothes?

Why were some of them carrying old people and children on their backs?

The suffering in their faces reminded him of Mr. Paul. Roy tried to turn and ask one of the Ray Riders what was happening, but the crowd's momentum swept him forward. As he moved with the others, the air filled with moans, soft and broken. Somewhere near him, a mother whispered to her crying son:

"It's only a few days, my son. Just a short visit to our homeland. Barzakh. Then you'll be back to your toys, your friends, your school."

Her words echoed in Roy's mind. *Barzakh? A short visit?* It felt more like a life sentence than a temporary trip. Roy could barely remember his homeland, though half his life had been spent there.

Then, pain.

Pain in Roy's legs.

In his hips. In his hands.

Pain—that was all that remained after hours of walking.

As the air grew colder, Roy began to shiver. The cold gnawed at him like a living thing. He could barely move his feet; they were frozen blocks beneath him. Finally, the mass of people arrived at an open field surrounded by metal fences.

The Ray Riders shouted:

"Move! Move!"

Roy staggered forward. He found himself face to face with another Ray Rider and asked:

"Where are we going?"

The Rider only barked:

"Move!"

But then, an older woman noticed Roy. She reached out; her face lined with sorrow.

"Son," she whispered.

"I am displaced, like others

Driven from our homes."

She wiped at her eyes with trembling fingers.

"I left everything...

My kitchen… my garden… my animals…

My heart is still back there."

She cried. Roy said nothing. He couldn't find the words.

Inside that encampment, there were a few scattered tents. Only a lucky few got inside. Most had to wait outside, shivering in the cold, hoping to exchange places later.

The twin sun sank lower, and the cold deepened, sharp as knives. Roy was lucky. He squeezed inside one of the tents, barely. The inside was no comfort. It was a breath warmer than outside, but there was no room to lie down. Only standing. Or sitting in tight circles, bodies pressed together. Despite the crowd, Roy still felt frozen. He had no coat. No blanket. Nothing.

He looked around and saw a man sleeping, his body wrapped in a thin blanket. Roy moved closer and sat beside him quietly. Without asking, he slipped his frozen hands and feet under the man's blanket, desperate for warmth.

The man stirred. He felt the ice of Roy's skin and opened one eye. His voice was hoarse:

"Where's your family?"

Roy answered quietly:

"I don't have. My mother died…when we crossed."

The man said nothing more. Roy leaned his head against the man's shoulder. And then, exhausted, he slept, a deep, heavy sleep.

By dawn, Nuro, Kato, a few friends, and several of Okasha's guards gathered in secret at Amara's grave. They were waiting for Fahd, but he hadn't arrived yet. As they stood there in silence, Nuro felt something warm.

A presence.

Her. He felt Amara beside them. If she were alive, she would have supported their plan.

Kato broke the silence, standing near the edge of the grave. He looked around at the others, then added softly,

"We're few, but I am prepared."

Nuro nodded, his gaze fixed on the fresh earth. *"It doesn't matter. What matters is, we're on the right side."* He took a slow breath. *"We won't seek a direct fight with the Ray Riders. No conflict. Just disruption."*

Kato raised a brow. *"So, what exactly are we doing?"*

Nuro answered: *"We'll ruin their plan. We board the* Fölkä Al-Orun *before the Crossers do."*

He looked each of them in the eye.

"Once you're aboard—don't leave. Not until you hear a word from me." *"They can't sail with us onboard. And we won't be alone."*

"Taziri will be there. Her father, too. And the Siddiq, *a man who, to many* Orunians, *carries more weight than my entire royal family."*

"If we get inside, the displacement will be delayed. Maybe even stopped."

"And then... Chad's slaves will have to negotiate with us."

A pause.

"And only then, we'll choose our next step."

Just then, the sirens blew. Everyone fell silent, listening. Then, Fahd appeared. Nuro stepped toward him.

"What's happening? The siren, why?"

Fahd's face was pale.

"The silos. They're burning. And they're about to explode."

"Father went there. I'm sorry to all of you...

But I won't be going to the harbor." "I have to go to the silos."

Kato spoke next. *"Me too. I'm with* Fahd.*"*

Then one of the others added, quietly:

*"*Nuro... *I'm sorry. My family lives just behind the silos.*

I have to get them out. Now."

He turned and ran. Nuro stood still. Everyone looked to him, waiting, waiting for his decision. But Nuro said nothing. He was thinking, torn. *Which was right? Which was wrong?*

Go with his brothers—to protect Orun from catastrophe?

Or go to the harbor—to protect the Crossers from exile?

He didn't know. The silence hung thick around him. Then someone else spoke:

"We should split.

Nuro, go with your brothers to the silos.

The rest of us will go to the harbor."

"If the explosion is controlled...

Join us later."

Nuro nodded. But as he turned, a deep guilt settled in his chest. Taziri. He was leaving her, leaving her there, to fight alone. Nuro couldn't forget Taziri. He had abandoned her once. He wouldn't do it again. But first—this.

Nuro, Kato and Fahd rode toward the silos on horseback. From two miles away, Nuro noticed; there were no visible flames, but something was wrong. As they drew closer, the sky behind the silos shimmered—not like wind, but like waves. Even the trees in the distance were trembling, blurred, as if hiding behind a veil of steam. The edges of the silos rippled, dissolving into ghostly vibrations.

Ahead, he saw his father Okasha with Chad, standing at a distance from the silos. As Nuro and Fahd approached, a strange scent reached them, sweet at first, like burnt toast.

They dismounted and joined their father. Okasha turned to glance at Nuro, then back to the silos, now slowly being swallowed by fire.

As they watched their future, grain, food, hope—burn, Okasha thought of the falling pearls in his Unabii. This was the second. The third is coming. But now, after losing Amara, everything became weightless.

Then Nuro spoke first:

"We're standing here watching the fire eat our next year's survival.
And we do... nothing?"

Chad answered with a dismissive smirk:

"We can't. What you're suggesting would cause a gas explosion. It could kill the rest of Orun's *people.*
Keep your wisdom to yourself."

Nuro narrowed his eyes.

"We must try something. Just watching is the worst choice."

Okasha raised his voice, cutting between them:

"Did you hear your brother?
Did you listen?"

"You're Crown Prince now. You should know;
Putting out a fire like this could cause a gas blast.
Doing nothing is the best option."

"And now we have a serious problem.
For this year.
For the next.
For the next generation."

Then Chad added, coldly:

"The Crossers did this.
People full of resentment.
They never deserved the dignity we gave them."

"They should return to their land—all of them.
Look what they've done! What more are we waiting
for?"

"We should care only for our people.
Only for Orunians.*"*

Nuro interrupted, voice sharp:

"I dare you to do it, even with your brainless slaves!"

Okasha raised his hand—Enough. Silence returned. Nuro's thoughts drifted to Taziri. He wanted to be by her side.

This title, this Crown, it wasn't for him. He should give it back.

But how? And when?

As fire continued to swallow the silos, meanwhile, near the harbor, in the hush of early sun, the Ray Riders stormed into the tents. They barked orders at the sleeping people:

"Move! Move!"

Outside, other Riders were already pulling down the tents, the cloth walls collapsing onto those still sleeping.

People screamed… ran, horrified.

Inside Roy's tent, where he had fallen asleep beside the blanket man, the noise jolted them awake. People stumbled and fell over each other. Roy and the blanket man stood quickly, circling a crying baby caught under the falling bodies, shielding him from being trampled. The Ray Riders kept pushing, shouting. They herded the crowds outside, toward the harbor. Roy stayed close to the blanket man as they moved with the tide of people.

At the harbor, two massive ships loomed above the crowd. The names were painted in bold letters across their sides:

Folká Al-Orun

They waited, engines rumbling. Between them bobbed a few small boats, tethered loosely.

The Ray Riders kept shoving. *"Move! Move!"*

Roy stumbled forward. In the crush of bodies, he saw an old man fall, pushed aside by the crowd. He fell into the freezing water between the dock and the ship's hull. Roy gasped, but no one moved to help him. The Ray Riders didn't even glance at him. They just kept pushing the others forward, over the man's drowning body.

Roy clenched his fists. *Do they know any other words besides "Move"?*

Near Roy, another man shouted:

"We have children! Old people! It's freezing!

We are not animals!"

The Ray Riders answered with blows. They struck him down and shoved the crowd harder.

"Move! Move!"

Roy was forced up the ramp of the second Fólká Al-Orun, the blanket man close behind. They stepped together aboard.

In just a few minutes, the two massive city-ships— Fólká Al-Orun, along with the smaller boats, were packed with Crossers, bodies pressed against each othters. Then, launched into the ocean, heading toward Barzakh, beyond the Panthalassic wall.

On the deck of the second **Fólká Al-Orun**, Roy and the Blanket Man managed to claim a narrow strip of space. They sat together, shoulder to shoulder, knees drawn in, their backs resting against the cold steel rail, silent, tense, watching the shoreline of Orun fade away. Then slowly, cold ruled the deck of Fólká Al-Orun.

Roy turned to the Blanket Man. *"I'll go below,"* he said.

"Maybe it's warmer there. Maybe I can find us a place."

The Blanket Man nodded.

"I'll wait here. If you find somewhere—save it for both of us, then come back to pick me up."

Just as Roy was about to leave, the Blanket Man stopped him.

"Wait." He pulled off his coat and handed it to Roy.

Roy blinked. *"But what about you?"*

The Blanket Man smiled faintly. *"Never mind. I'll cope."* The blanket man had only his thin shirt and a dirty blanket, nothing more. But he gave away his coat without hesitation.

He waited and waited…two hours passed, and Roy didn't return. Despite the brutal cold, the children on the deck played, their laughter sharp and high in the freezing air.

They didn't know. They didn't understand.

If they did—they would never have played.

> The Blanket Man hesitated. *Should I go down? Search for him? But what if Roy came back and didn't find me?* In a crowd of thousands, losing each other would mean losing each other forever.

So, he stayed. He cupped his hands to his mouth and shouted:

"Roy! Roy! Where are you?! ROY!" He called until his voice cracked.

Still standing in place, he shouted again, his eyes scanning the crowd on the deck, searching every face. Doubt gnawed at him. *Should I risk leaving the deck to search below?* He hesitated, took one step, and then stopped.

Finally, Roy appeared, breathless, climbing up from the lower deck. The Blanket Man rushed to him, didn't move far, just enough to meet him. He pulled him into a hug, as if he'd been missing him for decades.

"Where have you been?"

Roy shook his head. *"There's no space inside. Not even for a foot. Most of them are families with young children. We have to stay here."*

Roy shrugged off the coat, holding it out. *"Here. Take it back."*

The Blanket Man refused. *"Keep it. I'll manage with the blanket."*

They sat together, huddled for warmth, covering themselves as best they could. Roy leaned against him, his mind drifting.

Was it worth it? Was it worth crossing to Orun?

He had lost his mother on that journey—on the way to what was supposed to be a better life. Would it have been better to stay in Barzakh? To never leave? He thought of her now, the price he had paid. And now, returning, not as a man with dreams, but as a boy carrying sorrow.

At the edge of the horizon, the Panthalassic wall loomed. The same wall. The same towering mass of stone. It hadn't changed.

But Roy had.

Once, he had seen it with wonder. Now, only with oppression and injustice. As Folká Al-Orun moved away from the sun, the darkness of night swallowed the deck.

By the time they reached the Panthalassic wall, they passed through the gate, toward Barzakh, and the sun's last light was fading. That's when Roy noticed it.

A smell.

Foul.

Rotten.

Strange.

At first, he thought it came from the overcrowded mass of people, but they were all out in the open, sitting in the wind. It didn't make sense. He turned to the Blanket Man: *"I'll check."*

He rose, stumbling toward the ship's rail. His fingers touched the metal. It burned with cold, ice against his skin. He leaned over carefully and looked down.

The smell hit him harder. It was coming from the ocean. He saw bubbles rising everywhere, surrounding the ship, huge pockets of air, hissing and bursting as they broke the surface. It was as if the ocean itself were vomiting. The stench worsened. The bubbles grew larger, frothing wildly. Roy squinted toward the bow. One of the smaller boats had stopped, stuck right at the gate of the Panthalassic wall. Something was wrong. Deeply wrong.

Roy backed away from the rail. He hurried back to the Blanket Man. Roy felt something before he saw it. A sensation he had never felt before. It was as if a giant invisible hand reached inside his chest and clutched his heart. The smell grew stronger. It hit him like a slap. As their ship moved closer to Barzakh behind the wall, the smell changed, turning bitter, sulfurous.

It was that kind of scent that screamed: *Run. But run where?*

Roy and the Blanket Man tried to rest. They pulled the blanket around them, trying to steal a few moments of sleep. But that child nearby—the one crying without pause—kept screaming. Louder than the siren Roy remembered from his school. Finally, the Blanket Man muttered to the child:

"Please... stop... let us go in peace."

Then, suddenly—silence.

The crowded deck of Fólká Al-Orun fell utterly still.

No moans. No sobs.

Even the unstoppable child—silent. It wasn't peace.

It was fear.

Everyone was listening.

Then, Knock. Knock. Knock. Knock.

The whole ship vibrated. A deep, rhythmic thud. Like a giant hammer striking the ship's side.

Roy felt it in his bones. The vibrations ran up through the floor, into his chest. All around him, people froze. The ship shivered under the blows. They felt it, the sound of death knocking at their door. Roy turned to the Blanket Man. *"What's that?"* he whispered.

The Blanket Man's voice was low, steady, without fear:

"We are sinking."

For a moment, nothing. The words floated between them. Then the Blanket Man added, as if thinking aloud:

"Pressure...Pressure from outside. Crushing us."

Roy shook his head, trying to understand:

"How? How could that even happen?"

Before the question could leave his mouth, it happened. The balance shifted. Faster than a blink. The bow of the ship dipped violently downward. The deck tilted.

People slid toward the bow like marbles spilling off a table. Chaos exploded like fire over water. Screams tore through the night. Bodies ran—tripping, falling, clawing—toward the opposite side, to the ship's stern. Others threw themselves into the freezing water, panicking.

From below, people flooded out from the lower decks, pushing upward—climbing over others—fighting for space. Many never made it. They slipped. They fell into the black water.

Roy and the Blanket Man didn't move. They gripped the rail, holding on with everything they had.

And then Roy saw it.

The father of the once-screaming child grabbed his son and threw him into the ocean. The mother screamed—a sound sharper and louder than anything Roy had ever heard. She screamed louder than the boy's cry as he hit the water. Roy's legs tensed. He almost leapt after the child.

But he saw them—the parents themselves, following their son, diving into the freezing black.

The Blanket Man gripped Roy's arm.

"*Stay*," he said firmly.

As the bow rail dipped into the water, the ship's forward tilt slowed for a breath.

Then, without warning, **Folká Al-Orun** lurched violently to its right side—the opposite side from where Roy was holding the rail. The deck tipped hard. Screams rang out. Most people still on board were flung over the edge, swallowed by the ocean.

They vanished.

Gone, as if swallowed by quicksand. The life jackets didn't help. Nothing helped.

Roy heard the Blanket Man shouting:

"Hold on!

Hold the rail—tight!"

They clung to the rail, their feet hanging in empty air. Below them, the others disappeared, not a trace left behind.

The Blanket Man screamed:

"Don't jump! There will be a whirlpool.

Whatever happens—don't jump!"

Roy's hands ached. The rail froze his fingers. He stared toward the bow and saw what had become of the first ship. It was gone. Completely. The small boats, too, swallowed without a sound, without a ripple.

It was like falling into a hole punched into the ocean. Then, the lights of Folka Al-Orun went out.

Darkness. Thick. Total.

No shapes. No bodies.

Only the roaring sound of the dark waters and—Knock. Knock. Knock. The ship shuddered under the invisible blows. The frequency of the knocking grew faster. Harder. Death entered their door. Even the strongest swimmers vanished into the darkness. The ones who had leapt in first—all gone.

The ship wasn't sinking anymore. It was falling. Falling downward, into the deep.

Roy and the Blanket Man held tight, along with a few others. Their faces twisted in terror.

Suddenly, a huge man, frantic and desperate, lost his grip. He scrambled upward, his hand slipping. He grabbed the Blanket Man, clawing at him, climbing over him. Their combined weight wrenched the rail. The Blanket Man gasped, voice broken:

"I can't...

I can't hold both of us!

What's the use if I die too?"

The huge man looked at Roy. A look filled with a thousand unspoken words. A look of surrender. Of hopelessness.

Then, He let go. He fell. Vanished.

The fall of the ship sped up. Water rose, slapping against Roy's feet. Then his knees. Then his waist. The water kept rising.

Higher.

Higher.

The ship continued its slow, merciless fall into the deep. Now, only Roy and the Blanket Man remained. The waves battered them relentlessly, slapping their faces with cruel hands. Wave after wave, punishing them for refusing to let go. The water reached their chins. Their mouths. Their noses. The Blanket Man gasped for breath, then shouted:

"Climb over me!

Get onto the rail!

Go. Go!"

Roy hesitated, trembling from exhaustion. The Blanket Man shoved him with what strength he had left: *"Go now!"*

Roy moved. He wrapped his arms around the Blanket Man's neck, clinging for a moment. He rested there briefly, too tired to make another move, then whispered: *"You come with me."*

But the Blanket Man snapped: *"Go! I said Go!"*

Roy lifted his head. *"But, what about you?"*

The Blanket Man smiled faintly, even through the freezing water:

"I'll cope. Go."

Roy had heard those words from him once before—words that had saved him. He obeyed. Using the Blanket Man's shoulders, he climbed upward. His foot slipped. The Blanket Man grasped Roy's legs, pushing him with all his remaining strength toward the rail.

Roy landed on his stomach across the rail, gasping. He swung his legs over and stood. Wobbling. Shivering.

He turned back, reaching out, looking for the Blanket Man. To help him up. To pull him over the rail, too.

But he was gone. No trace.

Swallowed by the black ocean. Like quicksand. Like the thousands before him. Only the empty water stared back at Roy.

Then, the ocean calmed. The waves stopped. The rage withdrew, as if the ocean had swallowed enough flesh and was finally satisfied. Now, silence.

No more screaming.
No more voices.
No more life.

Fólká Al-Orun was almost entirely underwater now. The water lapped around Roy's legs—but it wasn't cold anymore. It was warm. Then, he heard it.

A voice.

Soft. Spreading everywhere. He turned to the right. The left. It repeated:

"Father...
Father..."

Roy knew that voice. He had missed it more than anything—his mother.

She had always called him *Father.*
Not Roy.
Not Son.
Just—*Father.*

It had been her special name for him. A tribute to another time—to his grandfather, who had also been named Roy. Something sacred between them. Even the neighbors, even his aunts, had picked it up, calling him *Father* when he was just a little boy.

Roy closed his eyes.

The calmness and warmth of her voice filled him. He let himself fall into it, let himself remember.

He was six years old again. The smell of the ocean drifted through the air. He stood barefoot on the shore, tiny and eager. His mother knelt beside him, smiling.

"I'll prepare the cactus fruit for you, Father," she said.

It was his first time tasting it. The cactus skin was covered with tiny spikes, dangerous. Inside, the flesh was sweet and sugary and filled with hard stones. He bit into it greedily, and one of the stones shattered his baby tooth. Pain flared. He cried, clutching his mouth.

But his mother had only hugged him tighter, whispering:

"Shall I show you a way to get your tooth back again?
Stronger. Bigger."

She took his hand and led him to the beach. There, under the burning sun, she sang a song he still remembered:

"Oh sun, oh little shining sun,
Take Father's baby tooth away,
And bring him a stronger, wider one,
A tooth big as a buffalo's!"

Then, she tossed his broken tooth into the sea.

"Wait," she said.
"The bigger tooth will come."

But it never came. The sun had broken its promise.

Now, standing on the sinking ship, Roy smiled. The memory burned clear. He could feel her with him. Right now.

As she always had been. Her warmth. Her arms were around him. All those lost memories—buried and locked away—had burst open.

The locks broken.

The covers lifted.

Everything was clear now. Roy stood alone on the dying ship, the last survivor. Calm. Unafraid. Not even tired. Her spirit fed him. She was near. So near he could almost touch her. He closed his eyes and let her hold him one last time.

At the harbor, Taziri's body lay still, unmoving. After being struck by the Ray Riders, she had lost consciousness. Her horse found her. He licked her face. He nudged her with his head, gently at first, then more firmly, trying to wake her.

Eventually, her body shifted, and she stirred. The horse turned, lowering himself slightly to let her climb on. Taziri sat up slowly. She looked around.

The harbor was empty. Her plan had failed.

All the Crossers had gone, departed. Vanished. She was alone. Helpless. No idea where to go or what to do.

Her father, missed.
Siddiq, nowhere.

She couldn't see them. Couldn't find anyone. The sadness was endless, trapped deep inside her. But her horse knew. He felt her pain—better than any human. He knew where to take her. He carried her to the secret place, her hidden Heaven. To the hidden plain between the two mountains.

No people. No eyes. No noise. Just silence.

When they reached the plain, she looked down toward Orun's Lake. And she saw him.

Chad.

He stood alone at the shore. She dismounted, quietly slid behind one of the trees, and watched him. He was wearing a black Asiago. He walked along the shore, gathering stones.

One by one, he tossed them into the lake, laughing. Smiling.

Taziri froze. *What madness is this? He should be with the silos, worrying about* Orun's *food, its people.*

But Chad kept going. He smiled wider. Smirked—pure evil across his face. He started whispering. At first, Taziri thought he was speaking to someone. But there was no one. He was talking to himself.

Then she saw the anointing horn in his hands. He uncorked it. Poured the oil over his face. It dripped over his eyes. His cheeks. His lips. Then he threw the horn aside.

Reached into his pockets. Pulled something out and fastened it onto both shoulders.

Taziri's heart pounded. This was no celebration. No ritual. This was madness. Madness dressed in triumph. She crouched lower behind the tree.

Chad suddenly paused. Then, he looked up, straight at her hiding place.

He knew. He sensed he wasn't alone.

His eyes were fixed on the trees.
Scanning.
Searching.

He mounted his horse. Began riding, slowly, toward her. Taziri turned around, back against the bark. She sat down, shivering…trembling.

Her hands shook. She whispered to her horse to be still. Her mind raced.

Should I stay and scream? Or should I run now?

She clenched her jaw. She had lost all sense of time. She would do both—if he got too close, she'd scream and run. Then she heard him. Getting closer. His horse's hooves brushing through the tall savannah grass.

Closer.
Closer.
She was afraid.

What if he kills me?
What if he buries me here?
In this secret place where no one would find me?

She closed her eyes. Breathed slowly. Tried to calm herself. The sounds stopped.

No movement. No voice.

Chad sat on his horse, silent, just outside her view. Then... his horse turned away. Chad spoke to it:

"Come. Let's go home."

Taziri waited. She heard the hoofbeats retreating.

Fading.

She didn't look back. She kept her eyes shut. She let out a quiet breath.

Pause.

Carefully, she turned her head. Just enough to part the grass and peer through. She saw him with her large eyes. Riding away, skimming over Orun's Lake.

Gone.

For now. The madness had passed. But only for a while.

On the cursed, falling ship, the darkness remained. Nothing had changed. Even when Roy closed his eyes, it was still the same darkness. He took a deep breath. The silence wrapped around him. But beneath his feet, he could feel it, the faint, trembling vibration of the ship's final struggle. Roy peeled off his useless lifejacket and threw it aside. He was ready now.

He stood still. Waiting.

Then, behind his closed eyelids, a brightness appeared.

Soft.
Calm.

A brightness not of panic, not of explosions, but of peace. Roy hesitated. Afraid....

Afraid that if he opened his eyes, the fragile light would vanish. Afraid that whatever waited for him beyond it would be darker than before. But he decided.

He opened his eyes.

It was not the sun.

It was not the *Lune*.

It was **Mr. Paul**.

Standing there in front of him.

Alive.
Smiling.
At ease.

No blood.
No wounds.
No broken face.
No torn scalp.

Just Mr. Paul—whole.

Exactly as Roy had never known him.

The same clothes. The same hair.

Everything was perfect.

Roy's tongue spoke:

> *"I'm really sorry.*
> *I'm sorry I couldn't bring you the water you asked for.*
> *I hope…. You aren't suffering anymore."*

Mr. Paul said nothing. He just smiled. Unchanging. Eternal. Then, the distance between them began to grow. Mr. Paul didn't walk. He didn't move his feet. He simply, shifted away. Sliding backward through the air, he was diving into a current no one else could see.

Roy's heart panicked. *I won't lose him again.* He stepped forward. He followed. Step after step, Roy walked along the rail under the water. The ship was tilting further, falling. The slope grew steeper with every step.

Roy quickened his pace.

Faster.
Faster.

Almost running along the water-covered rail to catch up.

Mr. Paul drifted toward the stern. Roy pushed harder. He reached the ship's giant propeller, massive, hanging high above the ocean.

But then, Mr. Paul vanished.
Like a mirage. Evaporated.

Roy staggered to a stop. Uncertain.

Was it real?
Was it an illusion?
Was it a reflection from the other world?
Was it a dying dream?

He didn't know.

And then, he saw it. Not a vision. Not a ghost.

A small boat.

One of the boats that had been trapped before, at the Panthalassic wall gate. It was still there.

Floating. Unaffected. Untouched. No boiling sea around it. No collapsing bubbles. Just calm water. The boat drifted steadily.

Waiting.

Roy's heart jumped inside his chest—and into the water. Roy couldn't swim. Even if he could, it wouldn't have mattered. He hit the water like a stone. He fell faster than the cursed falling ship itself. But Roy fought back. He slapped the water with his hands. Kicked with his legs, thrashed with everything he had.

He was a fighter. He refused to drown. But the ocean was stronger. It dragged him downward, pulling him under the surface. As he struggled blindly, something struck him hard. It was rough. Solid. He grabbed it without thinking.

A rope.

He clutched it with both hands. Pulled himself upward. The rope seemed to pull him too, dragging him back toward the surface.

He broke through. Sucked in a breath of salty air—and was immediately slapped across the face by the cold wind.

Then he heard a voice shouting:

"Swim!
Faster!
Before the whirlpool!"

Roy pulled at the rope, his muscles burning. It led to the floating boat—the one he had seen trapped at the gate. They were trying to pull him in.

But then, everything stopped. The rope stopped pulling. Roy's arms stopped pulling. Something yanked at him from below, from another direction. Something wanted to tear him in two.

The starving whirlpool. It pulled at him viciously, sucking him toward the ship's grave.

Roy's hands slipped. He sank again beneath the surface. The skin tore from his palms, leaving raw, bleeding flesh. He could no longer grip the rope with his hands. So, he clamped it between his teeth.

To the last standing tooth.

He bit down hard, refusing to let go. The rope strained. Pulled. Tore at his jaw. But still, he didn't let go.

They dragged him from the whirlpool, up toward the boat, toward the surface.

He broke through.

Gasped, another burning breath.

Still biting the rope, till he reached the rail of the boat. But he was too exhausted to climb. He dangled there, his body limp, his jaw locked tight around the rope.

Then small hands grabbed him. Dragged him over the side. Roy collapsed onto the floor of the boat, hitting the ground face-first. He lay there, unable to lift his head, his chest heaving, coughing up the burning saltwater from his lungs. He opened his burning eyes. Dozens of tiny feet surrounded him, small legs darting around.

But then, they scattered.

Roy blinked. Confused.

He looked down at his hands. There was no skin left. Only raw, exposed flesh. He sat up slowly. Leaned his back against the boat's rail, gathering his breath, feeling the world tilt and spin around him.

On land in front of the burning silos, Taziri's father approached Nuro and whispered something into his ear, news from the harbor. Nuro's heart clenched.

"Where is she now?"

Taziri's father shook his head. *"I thought you might know."*

Nuro whispered: *"I do."* He turned to Okasha. *"I need to check something in the city. I'll return."*

He mounted his horse and rode. He headed for the hidden place between the mountains, at the edge of Orun's Lake—*her place.*

The path was overgrown, long savannah grass brushing his legs, scratching him with thorns. He climbed. The plain had changed. The grass was taller, untouched, forgotten. At first, it seemed empty. Then, he saw her horse, standing alone. He pushed through the grass, hands parting the blades from his face.

He found her.

Taziri sat curled on the ground, knees pulled to her chest, arms wrapped tight.

Her face was pale. Dry. Her eyes red from crying.

Nuro sat beside her, shoulder to shoulder. He said nothing. He stared down at Orun with her. Then, a deep breath.

> *"I've decided to give my position back.*
> *I'm done.*
> *I don't want this... royal weight."*

Taziri said nothing. Then, quietly:

"It won't change anything."

Silence again. Longer this time. Then she spoke, voice cracked and low:

> *"I'll sail to Barzakh.*
>
> *I'll live with the Crossers.*
>
> *That's where I belong.*
>
> *Even if the radiation breaks me."*

She turned to him.

> "Nuro... *are you with me?*
> *Will you come with me?*
> *Escape all this? I'm serious."*

Nuro hesitated. He opened his mouth, *"I would..."*. But the word *radiation* echoed in his head. He thought of Amara. His mother. Dead. From radiation. From Barzakh. He paused. Then answered:

> *"What about our parents?*
> *Yours. Mine.*
> *They're old. They need us.*
> *Running away won't solve everything."*

Taziri exhaled hard. Then, softly:

> "Nuro...
> *I want to be alone."*

"I'm sorry.
I don't mean to be rude.
I just need time."

"I'll be alright."

Nuro stood. Backed away slowly, his eyes still on her, until he felt his back hit his horse. He mounted. He left.

No words. No goodbye.

Only silence.

As he rode behind the mountain, he passed Siddiq's home. The prayer mat was still there, but no prayers were on it.

No whispering. No movement.

The door was open. But the house…was empty.

On the rusty boat, Roy was shivering, while on land, the silos of Orun burned. He tried to warm himself with his own breath, blowing over the frozen flesh of his hands. Then he pulled his knees tightly toward his chest, hugging himself, trying to trap whatever warmth he had left. He blew between his arms and legs, curled into a tight ball against the rail of the small, rusty boat.

His eyes searched the deck.

Where did they all go? The ones with the tiny feet.

Why had they run away?

Roy pushed himself up, half-standing, his knees bent, his back curved like an old man. Still fighting.

He heard whispers from the other side of the boat. He moved toward them. The whispers grew louder, a mix of different voices, blending together into a soft murmur he couldn't understand. Then he saw them.

Children.

Dozens of them gathered in a tight circle. In the center, a man's foot is limp on the floorboards. The man lay face down, unmoving. Roy rushed forward, heart pounding. He slipped into the circle and knelt beside the man. He turned him gently onto his side—It was Siddiq—the wise man of Orun.

Alive. But barely.

Roy sat beside him. The cold gnawed at them mercilessly. They shivered together. The children had no blankets or clothes to spare, but they gave them what mattered most—their warmth.

They formed a wall around them. They pressed their tiny hands against Roy and Siddiq's frozen skin. They breathed warmth into them, a living, breathing shield. Little by little, warmth returned to their bodies.

Siddiq stirred first. He gathered his little strength and whispered soft prayers to the Creator. Then he turned his face downward, placing his forehead against the deck, and prayed sincerely.

Roy watched, puzzled. After all they had suffered, after all they had lost—*how could* Siddiq *give thanks?* But Roy said nothing. He simply watched. And in that silent watching, he tried to understand, just a little.

When Roy's body warmed enough to move, he began hugging the children one by one, tears streaming down his face.

"Thank you," he whispered.

"Thank you, my heroes."

When Siddiq finished his prayer, he hugged the children too, folding them all into one embrace with Roy. A quiet, trembling circle of survival. After a while, Roy asked the children:

"What happened?

Where's the captain of this boat?

Why are you stuck here?"

One of the older children answered:

"The engine stopped."

Another added: *"The captain and the crew took a rubber boat. He told us he would come back."*

Roy frowned. *"He left you here?"*

The children shook their heads.

"No. He said he would return."

Roy looked at them, at their wide, trusting eyes. And he smiled, even though he was sad. Then he turned to Siddiq and asked, his voice sharp with exhaustion:

"So... what do we do now?

We've got a dead engine, a broken ship, and a sucking whirlpool in front of us."

Siddiq's voice came calm, unwavering: *"We sail."*

Roy stared at him, exploding.

"What? Is that a joke?

We don't have a captain. We don't have a crew.

We have no maps, no direction, nothing!

Who's going to sail us? The Creator?!"

Silence.

Siddiq didn't like the tone. He waited. Then asked softly: *"Tell me, Roy, can you swim?"*

Roy paused. *"No."*

Siddiq nodded slowly.

> *"Then how did you end up here, on this boat, when thousands of stronger swimmers drowned?"*

Another silence. Roy's mind searched for answers.

A mental block.

Then he mumbled: *"I... I tried to swim... and then I..."*

Siddiq stopped him.

> *"You tried.*
>
> *That's all.*
>
> *Now it's our turn."*

Roy had no more words. He looked away, refusing to argue further.

But Siddiq wasn't finished.

> *"Bring me to the wheel."*

Roy blinked. ***"What?"*** ***"Bring you to the wheel?"*** Roy's mind couldn't process it. *A blind man—at the helm of a dead ship?* Roy didn't understand. But he obeyed. He helped Siddiq to the back of the boat. There, an old wheel, a single rusted gear, one key.

Siddiq placed his hand on the wheel and smiled.

> *"Roy, son, you are my navigator now.*

You are my eyes.

We will sail north."

Roy hesitated. *"And where is north?"*

Siddiq tilted his head.

"Put the Panthalassic wall directly at your back."

Roy turned, aligning his body.

"Now look up at the stars

Can you find the Dipper?"

Roy's eyes scanned the sky. So many stars, random, chaotic, endless. *"I don't know what I'm looking for."*

"Take your time," Siddiq said gently.

"Search for a shape—like a saucepan."

Minutes passed. Then Roy pointed. *"I... I think I see it."*

The children burst into cheers. They jumped, clapped, and wrapped their arms around him, as if Roy had won a championship.

Siddiq smiled.

"At the outer edge of the Dipper are two bright stars.

They're pointers. See them?"

"Yes."

"Draw a line between them—extend it forward.

It will point to a single, bright star."

"That's Polaris," Siddiq said softly.

"The North Star."

"It marks our way."

Roy squinted. Then, he smiled.

"I found it.

I don't need more time. It's there."

Siddiq added:

"To be sure, Polaris is part of a smaller dipper.

It may appear above or below the larger one.

Can you see it?"

"Yes," Roy answered immediately.

The children danced, flew, and hugged Roy as if he had called down the sky itself. For a moment, all the suffering was forgotten.

Siddiq stood with one hand on the wheel.

"That," he said, *"is our direction.*

That is our future, but we wait.

We wait until the monster and his servant sleep..."

He meant the whirlpool and the rotten bubbles. And then, they would sail.

In front of Siddiq's door, Nuro was standing, searching, waiting for him to appear. The house was silent. Empty. The prayer mat lay untouched beside the old palm. No sign of life. Then, he heard footsteps. Kato approached, face pale, breathless.

"*Is* Siddiq *inside?*"

Nuro stepped toward him. "Kato, *tell me, what happened?*"

"*Wrong question,*" Kato snapped.
"*Is he inside?*"

Nuro's voice hardened. "Kato. *Answer me. What happened?*"

Kato inhaled sharply, his hands trembling.

"*Those Ray Riders… they're evil.*
They acted without orders.
They did it themselves."

Nuro shouted: "Kato*! Speak clearly! Enough of this, what happened?!*"

Kato swallowed hard, then finally said it:

"*They took them all.*
The Crossers.
Everyone, children, elders.
All departed"

"*At the harbor… it was chaos.*
Siddiq *was hit. No one has seen him since.*
Taziri *too. She was injured.*
Her father… others…"

Kato trailed off.

Nuro was silent, listening—Kato noticed, the veins in his eyes thickened, branching toward his pupils. His jaw locked, teeth grinding audibly. Kato could see the muscles in his brother's arms tighten, his hands curling into fists.

Suddenly, Nuro turned. He mounted his horse and rode like a flaming arrow down to the gates of Okasha's home. His horse burst forward so fast that the guards didn't have time to stop him.

He galloped across the courtyard, past stunned servants, toward Chad's room.

"CHAD!"
"CHAD!"
"CHAD!"

His voice roared through the stone corridors, vibrating the old walls like thunder. He reached Chad's door. Dismounted. Kicked it open. Inside, Chad turned, caught mid-thought, surprised.

"What have you done?!" Nuro's voice shook the air. *"Speak! NOW!"* He didn't wait. He grabbed Chad by the arm, ripped him out of the room, threw him through the shattered doorway, and pushed him out with both hands.

"GET OUT!"
"Can you feel it now?!
Taste it?!
GO! Anywhere! There's no place for you here!"

Chad stumbled. Paused. He turned, voice eerily calm: *"What happened, brother?"*

Nuro stormed toward him again.

"What happened?!
Ask your headless slaves!
Your soldiers!
Ask them what they did at the harbor!"

"Even Siddiq... our Siddiq... was hit."

Chad didn't flinch. *"They deserved it. They betrayed us."*

"STOP!" Nuro shouted.
"I withdraw everything.
All your powers.
You are DONE."

Chad bowed slightly. *"No problem, brother. I forgive you." "We are still brothers. In soul and blood."* He turned and walked away.

Nuro stood alone. His heart was pounding. His blood was still boiling. And then, a thought struck him.

Headless soldiers.

The words he had just spoken...He had heard them before. He had seen them. The second Unabii. People without heads. Standing on spears. The Ray Riders. It was them. But the rest of the vision...was still unclear...Still waiting.

As Chad passed through the main gates, the guards noticed something strange. He was smiling.

By sunrise, silence had spread across the rusty boat. The children slept. Even Siddiq's whispers had faded. Stillness settled over the deck.

Then, soft thuds.

Left side. Right side. Below the hull.

Like birds falling from the sky.

Roy looked over the rail. Life jackets surfaced, floating silently.

Then, bodies. Dozens. Hundreds.

Thousands.

They rose in waves, until the ocean itself became a silent grave.

Siddiq spoke, his voice wrapped in sorrow:

"The monster is sleeping.

We must move."

Roy nodded. He moved to the anchor, still caught at the edge of the Panthalassic wall. He pulled it up with trembling hands, freeing the boat from the gate.

Siddiq reached out, searching the control panel for the key. As he felt along the surface, his hand unintentionally moved the gear into the 'N' position while still searching.

Roy noticed and said gently, *"The key is on your right."*

Siddiq's fingers shifted, and when he turned the key, the engine roared to life. The sudden sound cracked the silence like a whip. Children stirred, blinking awake.

In the water, the bodies clustered, drawn toward the noise, toward the warmth of the boat—as if begging for one more chance. Siddiq gripped the gear and pushed it forward. The boat began to move.

"Slightly left." Roy instructed.

The boat turned. Slowly. Carefully. It sailed through the bodies, cutting between the dead. Roy looked at the children—now awake, now watching. He couldn't let them see. He needed to distract them.

So, he stood tall and called out:

"All right!

Who's the oldest one here?"

No answer. They were still blinking away sleep. Then, he asked again: *"How old are you?"* One by one, they responded, until he reached the oldest: *Nine.*

Roy smiled.

"Perfect.

We're doing something important today.

We need guardians for this boat."

"We need a new captain and a new navigator.

Anyone interested?"

A small hand shot up. Roy nodded.

"All right, just one question to begin..."

He paused.

"What would make you the happiest person in Orù.. *"*

Roy stopped himself…Orun…

He shouldn't have said it. Not now. Not to them. He cleared his throat, quickly corrected:

"I mean…mm…What would make you the happiest person of all time?"

The boy answered instantly:

"My chick."

The deck erupted in laughter. Roy grinned.

"Your chick? Why?"

"Because he thinks he's a duck." More laughter. Roy laughed too.

"Ambitious bird! Can he fly?"

"No."

"Dance?" "Kind of." "What color?"

"Brown."

Roy raised his eyebrows.

"Brown?

That's rare.

I thought chicks were yellow."

"He was brown," the boy insisted proudly.

Roy chuckled. *"Tell us something else about your chick."*

The boy's smile faded slightly.

"I...

I wish I still had him.

I was sad when he died."

The laughter faded. A quiet pause settled over them. Then Roy lifted his voice again: *"Congratulations. You're hired."*

The children clapped. Some cheered. Roy pointed to the sky.

"See that star? That one up there?

That's Polaris.

That's where we're going."

He turned to the boy.

"You're our navigator now.

That's your star.

We'll sail straight toward it, until we reach the land beneath it.

If we drift off course, you tell us. Deal?"

The boy nodded, proud and serious. He kept his eyes fixed on the star. Roy turned back toward the ocean. The bodies were behind them now. So were the fallen ships. So was the monster. They were moving forward.

He looked back at the children:

> *"Time to sleep again. Even our navigator needs rest."*
>
> *"The Polaris journey needs energy."*

The children settled once more, huddled close, under the stars.

Professor Casablanca, who had once been Roy, paused a little, then smiled softly, despite the tragedy he had lived through. He said:

"The faces of the children...

The joy on their faces, it was priceless."

Then, as if the ocean had heard him, the world around us changed. The clouds vanished. The waves grew still. The air turned warm again. And the bitter scent of foam disappeared. The message from the deep ocean was received. The ocean was calm now.

Professor Casablanca folded his hands and said:

"I hope you understand now what happened to the ships."

"There were no monsters.

No magic."

One of us raised a hand and said:

"Greedy Chad. It was him, right?"

The professor smiled but gently shook his head.

"I'm not judging. I'm just a storyteller.

I told you the story exactly as it happened."

Then he leaned forward.

"Two things happened to the fallen ships."

"Chad followed one rule and broke another."

"First, he followed the rule of leaving nothing behind.

No bodies.

No accusations.

No guilt."

"Second, he broke the law of Archimedes."

"He changed the buoyancy of water—by mixing it with methane gas."

"In other words, he transformed the water at the gate of the Panthalassic wall into air—or worse than air. Into methane."

"And so, the ships didn't sink. They fell. Like stones dropped through a hole in the ocean—their fall created a sucking whirlpool that dragged down everything left on the surface."

He continued:

"The hyperloops beneath the water, which were once used to carry food and gas between Orun *and Barzakh...*

But after the attacks, since Nuro *was born, they were abandoned."*

"Chad repurposed them. He used the pipelines inside them to pump methane gas into the ocean, right behind the Panthalassic wall."

"Methane has a density lower than air, and much lower than water."

"He turned the ocean into something that couldn't hold ships. So, they collapsed. Instantly."

"Those bubbles…
that smell…
It was all methane.
And methane, as you may know, smells like rotten eggs."

I raised my hand.

"What about Mr. Paul?

Was he… an illusion?"

The professor paused. Then smiled again.

"Illusion and reality—they are both just perception."

He leaned back and continued:

"A bee can't see red. Its retina isn't sensitive to that wavelength.

But it sees ultraviolet patterns on flowers that guide it to nectar."

"A cow can't see red either. To it, red is just gray."

"So, if a bee or a cow told the others, 'Hey, I see a red flower,' they'd think it was mad, a wizard, a heretic. Or just hallucinating."

"Even though red exists…it's simply beyond their perception."

He looked out at the waves.

"When I told the part about the Lune falling over my school... I saw Mr. Paul. Standing with us. Right there."

He pointed to the same spot where his eyes had been fixed a moment earlier—the place where I had thought he saw a ghost. Then he continued, his voice softer:
"I'm still not sure that's his real name. But I saw him."

"My eyes and my brain saw him many times."

"I know, part of it was post-traumatic stress.

A flashback.

A projection.

But he was... my guide.

He led me to the rescue boat.

He helped me survive."

"And since then...

I've seen him again."

Then he changed the subject.

"But enough of me. Let's return to Nuro's *second Unabii."*

He stood, drew a simple diagram on the stones of the Panthalassic wall.

"The people without heads?

That was the Ray Riders."

"The people without hearts?

The suffering Crossers."

"The eggs?

The methane bubbles—rotten-smelling and deadly."

"The blue desert? ..... That was the ocean."

"The long curtain? .... The Panthalassic wall."

"The two sliding plates? The ships."

"And the toy Chad *played with? It represented the pipeline inside the hyperloop. In the vision, he was blowing air into it. In real life—it was methane."*

After we sailed with the rusty Boat, I found myself watching Siddiq. He was sitting quietly, hands raised, whispering prayers. He was thanking the Creator. And I was... provoked. *Thanking Him? For what?*

For being expelled like insects? For falling into the ocean like stones?

It made no sense. Finally, I asked:

"Why do you thank Him? After all this?"

Siddiq turned his face toward the horizon, his voice soft:

"Son... life is short. Shorter than you can imagine.

It's shorter than the time between sunset and sunrise."

"Your whole life is just a visit. A brief stop in a foreign home."

"That home… is Earth….

So, remember, before you leave it: your life is only a short visit."

"Be a kind visitor. Leave in peace.

And don't be mean."

I shook my head.

"It's easy to be kind.

But thankful? That's different. They're not the same."

"What about loss? What about the unknown?

What are you even thanking Him for?"

Siddiq answered simply:

"For our fate."

Then he paused. The silence stretched.

"It already happened," he added.

I stared at him. *"What do you mean? Are we living in the past?"*

He nodded slowly. *"Yes."*

"But how?"

Siddiq's voice was calm, like the ocean:

"What your eyes see now… are flashbacks from your past life.

Everything has already happened.

Everything is written."

I leaned closer, struggling to understand.

"But… I still have choices.

I can change things.

I can act.

How can that be, if it already happened?"

He smiled faintly.

"You already changed it."

"That's why we're here.

On this boat.

For a reason. For a purpose."

"But you don't remember. It all happened long ago."

"You just forgot."

"The forgetting… is part of the visit."

"But we don't lose it forever.

Sometimes, the truth leaks through.

In flashes. In glimpses."

"Sometimes… in a Unabii."

I was quiet. Then I asked: *"Why do we forget our fate?"*

Siddiq replied:

"We don't forget. Not completely.

It's buried inside us, locked and sealed."

"But sometimes... something opens the door.

A dream.

A word.

A pain...."

"And when your visit ends, everything will be revealed."

"The blindness will lift.

The cover will fall away."

The
Wedding

UNABII #

Life had changed in Orun. Summer came. The Crossers left. They took with them their scent, their memories, and something else.

Joy.

The joy that once drifted through Orun's streets, schools, and homes along the shores of its lake…was gone as if they had carried it all with them into the deep water. Drown.

Life continued in Orun, but a lifeless life. Never the same.

Meanwhile, Roy, the children, and the Siddiq had arrived in Barzakh after three days of sailing. For the children, it was a new world. But Siddiq, the blind man, moved through it as if he'd known it before. As if he had lived there in another life.

On the land of Orun and inside Nuro's Mind, something was growing. A feeling. He was missing her. Again, and again. Deeper and deeper. But something else was trapped, a thought that refused to let him rest. It had circled in his mind for days, nights, weeks. So, he decided to go to her. To Taziri's home. That thing had to be said.

First obstacle: Leith.

Her horse stood alone, tied to that tree at the gate of her home, blocking the way like a jealous guardian. Nuro hesitated. He approached slowly. Then, stopped at a safe distance. They stared at each other—man and horse.

Silent.

Tension hung in the air like dust. Only jealousy could be smelled.

Finally, Nuro gathered his courage.

"Hey, Leith... *It's all right. I don't know why you hate me."*

He added.

"I don't know if you understood my words or not, but it would be nice if you stepped a little to the side so I can pass. Come on, tsk tsk tsk."

Leith moved, Nuro smiled.

But not in the way Nuro hoped. He turned his back to Nuro. Lowered his head. Preparing to kick.

Nuro backed up, annoyed.

"So... that's how you want it.

But for your knowledge, Taziri... *this girl...*

She's going to be my wife. So, you'd better start accepting it."

He said it. Out loud. And Leith exploded. He pawed the ground furiously, snorted so loudly that Taziri heard it from inside the house. She ran outside in alarm. Nuro stepped back again, eyeing the lead rope nervously. If it snapped, it wouldn't end well for him.

Taziri arrived and smiled.

"What are you two doing out here, my bears?"

Nuro said nothing. Leith immediately calmed as Taziri approached, stroking his face with both hands.

"*Why are you standing so far away?*" she asked Nuro.

"*Because of him,*" Nuro said, pointing.

"*Who?* Leith? *What do you mean?*"

"*He… he wants to kick me. I swear! Remember, I said it, you heard him snorting!*"

Taziri laughed gently.

"He *would never hurt anyone, especially not the ones I like. His heart doesn't know hate.*"

Nuro raised a brow. "*But his heart knows jealousy.*"

They both burst into laughter.

Taziri shook her head. "*No, I don't think so.*" *She turned to* Leith. *"Right, my panda? You're not jealous, are you?"*

She buried her hands in his mane. Then looked to Nuro

"*Come*, Nuro. *I'm here. It's all right.*"

"*Yes, but why is he giving me his back?*" Nuro asked.

"*Because I'm playing with his mane,*" Taziri said, grinning.

"Come, *just touch his back gently, from behind, so he knows you're there.*"

Nuro approached slowly, eyes locked on Leith's. But the moment he got close, Leith whipped his head around and tried to bite him.

Taziri doubled over with laughter. "Leith! *What are you doing?!"* She laughed harder. Then paused. Then laughed again, even louder.

Nuro threw up his hands. *"You saw that! He tried to bite me! Taziri, believe me, I'm not making this up. Well...he doesn't want me coming in today."*

"*Oh, come on,*" Taziri said, still laughing.

"*He'll let you in.*

He just wants me to take him for a walk. I haven't done that in days."

Nuro exhaled, finally relaxed. Then he said softly: "Taziri..."

She met his eyes. Something shifted.

He continued: "*I'm going to Barzakh. Would you come with me?"*

Taziri blinked. Then smiled.

"*Yes. A hundred percent yes. But... how?"*

She looked down at the ground.

"*I mean... my father won't accept. You know how strict our traditions are, especially among the Amazigh."*

She traced a pattern in the dirt with her foot.

Nuro nodded. *"That's why I came today."*

Taziri smiled but stayed silent. Still looking down. Inside her chest, fireworks were going off, a joy she'd never felt before.

Nuro continued:

"I've thought about our parents, too. We still have the hyperloops. They've been abandoned for years... but I'll ensure they're repaired. With the hyperloops, it'll take just minutes to go to Barzakh and back.

No more sailing. No flying."

"Also... one more thing."

"What?"

"The Crossers. They must return. I'm working with your father and other leaders.

But one thing at a time."

He paused again. Taziri stepped closer.

"What else? Keep going, Nuro.

You just made me the happiest person in all of Orun."

He looked at her gently. *"I missed you. More than I ever imagined."* Then added, shyly: *"Also... I need a hug."*

She smiled. *"Only one hug?"*

"Thousands," he said. *"But I can't. There's an obstacle between us. You saw it. I don't want to get kicked or bitten today."*

Taziri laughed. *"Then I have an idea. Wait."*

She walked over to the large tree where Leith was tied. With her index finger, she tapped gently against the trunk.

Tap. Tap. Tap

Then turned back and smiled.

Nuro blinked. *"What was that? Why did you tap the tree?"*

"If I ever can't hug you—for any reason—I'll tap like this on the tree."
"And when I do that, it means: I hugged you."

"That tapping will be our code. Just for us. A secret."

Nuro smiled. *"A secret?"*

"Yes."

"Well, not anymore," he joked, looking at Leith. *"He saw it. He heard it."*

They both laughed. Nuro took a deep breath. *"I think you should take* Leith *for that walk now...while I talk to your father."*

Taziri raised an eyebrow, narrowed her eyes. *"About what?"*

"It's a... men's thing," Nuro said, smirking. *"Go now."*

"Nuro, my father's not home."

"What?"

She laughed. *"What man, huh?"*

"Where is he?"

"I don't know. But I guess he'll be back soon."

"Then I'll wait," Nuro said. *"Go now."*

"All right, all right, my brown bear." she said with a grin.

After Nuro met Taziri's father, it was the first time he had felt truly happy since his mother Amara's death. That lightness followed him as he made his way to Fahd's room, where all his brothers, Chad, Fahd, and Kato, had gathered.

On the way, Nuro made a decision. He would speak his truth out loud. He would tell them, finally, that he intended to return the Crown Prince title. To give it back to Fahd or even Chad. It was the perfect chance.

When Nuro entered the room, Chad was sitting directly before him. They hadn't spoken since their last conflict.

Nuro looked at him. Chad didn't meet his gaze. He kept staring at the ceiling. Nuro walked closer. He reached out his hand. Chad took it. They shook hands as if nothing had ever happened. Then Nuro stepped into the center of the room and said:

"Brothers."

All eyes turned to him, except for Kato, who was, as always, distracted by something else.

"Kato," Nuro said sharply. "I want to make a statement."

He paused.

"*I've decided, ..*"

But Chad cut him off.

"*Stop. Stop. Stop.*"

Chad raised a hand.

"Before you say anything…I have something too."

Nuro looked confused. Then Chad stood up, smiling.

"I want to gather us again, like the old days. Just the four of us."

"I've planned a raying trip on the Gerridion."

Fahd nodded. "That's… nice."

Nuro added: "I think that's a great idea."

Chad continued:

"No royal talk. No politics. Just us. Like before.

Brothers in blood and soul."

Nuro hesitated. He considered saying it anyway. But then he thought better of it. *Maybe I would say it later. On the Gerridion. When things are more relaxed.*

Then Kato looked up. "Wait, am I even invited?"

Chad laughed.

Of course! Because someone has to stay behind to guard the bait and krill, right? Who else would guard them while we're out there?"

They all laughed. Kato rolled his eyes. *"Idiots. The all of you."*

Later, Fahd leaned toward Nuro and whispered: *"What was the statement you were going to make?"*

Nuro smiled faintly. *"You'll hear it on the Gerridion."*

Fahd raised an eyebrow. *"Doesn't sound like anything serious."*

Nuro shrugged. *"That's what it is."*

After his brother's meeting, Nuro entered his room and stood there, still. Something felt... strange. He couldn't explain it.

He wasn't happy. He wasn't sad. The feeling wasn't just in his heart. It was everywhere, inside every part of his body.

Something thick, but quiet.

He started to worry. *What is this feeling? Why does it feel so deep? Am I ill? Sick?*

He sat on the edge of his bed, retracing his day, replaying conversations, steps, meals, and silence. Maybe he missed something. But it wasn't memory. It wasn't a moment. It felt like something that hadn't even happened yet. The heaviness pulled at his body, dragged him down. He fell asleep.

Unabii#

The same vision. The same Unabii he had seen since birth. But now, more detailed. More motion. More... urgent.

Nuro looked at his hands. They were his, but not his skin. The scars were the same. The lines. The shape. But the skin wasn't his.

Then—The giant bird.

Then—The cave. The suffocating mountain air.

Old air.

Stagnant.

Heavy with time.

Days passed inside that cave, or maybe no time at all. Time stood still in the cave.

Then—the door opened.

Then—the free fall. Plunging toward Earth.

Heart racing. Breath gone. #

The Unabii ended, and Nuro woke up. Sweating. The fear inside the Unabii pulled him out. He couldn't go deeper. He had seen this Unabii dozens of times across his life. But never like this. This time, it felt closer.

Heavier.

He looked out the window. The first sun had barely moved, not even half an hour had passed. But inside the Unabii, it felt like days. The heaviness returned. Pulled at his eyes again. And again, he slept.

Unabii#

Same vision. Same rhythm.

Now—standing on a swinging, tilting sphere. His hands in cuffs.

Dragged upward—into the sky.

Then—vomiting. Coughing up saltwater.

Then—the cave.

But now, inside the cave, everything was upside down. Walking across spikes. The pain beneath his feet.

Then—the fall again.

And the landing—but on a cloud.

Then—images. Flashes.

A hand. Reaching. Helping.

A face.

A sad face. #

Nuro woke again. Staring. Breathing slowly. His mind tunneled in on the final image: That sad face of that man. The one who saved him. He could still remember him clearly:

Beard.

Sad.

No expression. No words.

Just a face.

And Nuro wondered, *who was he?* The heaviness now felt like tons pressing down. It wasn't a feeling. Not just Unabii. He knew it now. It was a warning, a signal.

Something was coming. Something would happen. And it was near. Closer than ever before.

A few days later, the raying trip began. Nuro, along with Fahd and Kato, made their way to the harbor. The **Gerridion**— the Water Strider boat was waiting for them. Chad was already on board, making final preparations. One by one, the brothers climbed aboard. Chad stood behind the wheel. Fahd took his place at Chad's right, while Nuro and Kato sat toward the back.

Chad looked out at the ocean, then turned to Fahd.

"I still remember it like it was yesterday… the day Nuro *was born.*

We were on a trip with the Dragon that day.

I was terrified we'd fall. I've never ridden in a Dragon again since."

Fahd smiled. "Maybe you have a phobia?"

"Could be," Chad replied, chuckling. *"But ever since, I've hated flying. The air feels wrong. The ocean is better. I trust it more, especially with the Gerridion."*

Nuro smiled quietly as he listened. Soon, the boat launched, skimming fast over the water. So fast that Kato and Nuro tightened their seatbelts like they were about to fly. The **Gerridion** skimmed above the waves at impossible speed. They crossed thousands of miles in what felt like the speed of the voice. Soon, they reached a spot just a few feet south of the

Panthalassic wall. Chad slowed the Gerridion, then dropped the anchor and leaned over the echo sounder.

Nuro and Fahd followed his eyes to the screen.

"*There*," Chad said.

"*Those large shapes… those are Mantas.*"

He reached for a bottle of fish oil and began pouring it into the water, spreading it across the ocean's surface.

Nuro leaned toward Fahd. *"What's* Chad *doing?"*

"*The fish oil attracts them,*" Fahd explained. "*They live deep down, and they're shy. But they're powerful. And intelligent. Sometimes they need a push to wake up the beast inside them.*"

Kato grinned from the back. "*Good luck with your Calamari. I'll stay here and eat.*" They all laughed.

Chad began to suit up. Nuro watched every movement closely. Chad pulled on his swimming suit, secured arm braces on both arms, then attached transparent lassos to either side. Fahd stood in front of him, running final checks. He adjusted the lasso attachments, ensuring the loops were snug and stable. He tapped both red ejection buttons on Chad's arm braces, testing the release mechanism.

Suddenly, Chad paused, his eyes on the screen.

"*Wait… wait… that's it.*"

The radar was shifting. A large, moving form appeared on the black screen.

"See that?" Chad shouted.

"It's massive!"

A white structure was rising on the screen, wings spreading.

"That's at least 23 feet, wingspan."

Fahd squinted. *"I think it's a Manta."*

But Chad cut him off, excited.

"No, look at its speed. Look.. That's not a Manta. Look at its front. Narrow. Long."

He leaned in. *"It's a devil. I'm sure of it."*

Nuro tried to take it all in. Too much information. Too fast. The creature disappeared from the radar. Chad leapt to the edge of the boat, scanning the water.

"Did you see it?" Fahd called.

"Not yet," Chad answered. *"It should appear soon."*

Then Chad placed a hand on Nuro's shoulder and pointed. *"There,"* he whispered. *"That's it. The Devil Ray."*

Fahd's eyes widened.

"I've never seen a Devil Ray that big."

"I told you," Chad said. *"It's a Devil Ray."*

Fahd tossed a handful of krill—**impregnated with Gravitron**—into the water.

Nuro turned to him. *"How can* Chad *be sure it's a Devil Ray?"*

Fahd shrugged.

> *"He says it's because of the horns. They look like a devil. That's where the name comes from."*

"So… are they dangerous?"

> *"No. Not unless provoked. They're shy. But when they're triggered, they become… something else."*

He held up the krill in his palm.

> *"This is the trigger. The key… to set the beast inside them free."*

Nuro nodded slowly. Below the surface, the Devil Ray approached the krill. Its mouth opened wide. Chad waited. The moment the ray began to feed, Chad threw both loops into the water, each loop aimed at a horn. Perfect catch. He pulled sharply. Then, he jumped.

The Devil Ray dove. Fast. Dragging Chad beneath the surface. Eight seconds later, Chad surfaced. He lay across the back of his ray, calm, effortless.

Then, with stunning speed, he rose out of the water like the flying fish breaking the surface. He flew over the Gerridion, soaring above his brothers, and splashed down on the other side, soaking them all.

Kato shouted: *"Hey, Chad! Enough! I told you to leave me out of this!"*

But it was too late. It had become Chad's show. He continued gliding across the ocean's surface, cutting through the waves like a blade. At the edge of their line of sight, he banked hard to the right, the wing of his ray skimming low, sending a mist of seafoam into the air. Then, he turned. Straight back toward the Gerridion. A direct line.

Nuro tensed. "Fahd... *what's he doing?*"

Fahd didn't answer. Just smiled.

"Fahd... *he's approaching us. This crazy* Chad..."

Still, Fahd said nothing.

"Fahd*! He's going to crash into us!*"

Even Kato saw it now. He jumped into the water, panicked. Nuro grabbed Fahd's arm, trying to pull him with him into the ocean. But Fahd didn't move. Nuro jumped alone.

Then, just centimeters before impact, Chad performed a parallel roll, releasing the loops from his arm braces, sliding off the ray in perfect control. The ray curved away. Chad landed, triumphant.

Fahd burst out laughing.

"*Perfect! That was perfect! I sent our brothers into the water!*"

From the sea, Nuro and Kato shouted: "*Both of you are idiots!*"

Kato added: "*But... that was exciting.*"

Fahd helped them both back aboard the Gerridion, except for Nuro. He stayed in the water.

And then, the ocean changed. What unfolded around Nuro felt like something from heaven. No words had yet been invented to describe what they saw. No eye had ever witnessed it before.

Silence.

Even Kato was speechless.

Rays. Dozens of them. Maybe hundreds.

Different types. Different colors.

Some of them were even glowing. They were dancing, spinning, and gliding through the water in perfect rhythm. A musical symphony without sound. All of them are swimming around Nuro.

Then, a large one approached.

Thick body. Rounded tail.

Fahd shouted:

"*Swim away!*

Get out of there!"

Nuro didn't move. His eyes were locked on the ray. It circled him, then dove into the deep.

Fahd was frantic:

"Nuro*! What's wrong with you? Are you deaf?*"

"That was an electric ray! A torpedo!

You could've been sent to heaven."

Nuro looked up at him calmly. *"I already am...in heaven."*

Fahd blinked. Then helped him back onto the Gerridion.

As Nuro climbed aboard, he asked: *"How did they gather around me like that?"*

Fahd answered:

"Like I told you, they're the most intelligent sea creatures.

But shy. They communicate through chemicals, through subtle cues.

They speak... without sound."

Nuro nodded. Then pointed toward Chad. *"And that one? That stingray your brother rides, how does he manage that?"*

Fahd answered:

"Stingrays are almost impossible to ride. They don't have horns. And they defend themselves with venomous spines on their tails. One strike can perforate your skin."

"That's why we have only one Stingray Rider in all of Orun."

They both turned to look at Chad. At that moment, Nuro noticed something odd. Chad was moving his lips.

Silently.

"Chad... *you alright?*" Nuro asked.

"*Yes*," Chad replied, without looking. "*I'm singing.*"

The moment passed. The rays began to scatter. Then, as the torpedo ray disappeared, Chad tossed more fish oil into the ocean. Then, more krill, Gravitron-treated. A shadow began to rise from the depths. Nuro turned to Fahd, who was already preparing for his next dive.

"*Jump!*" Nuro shouted. "*It's coming up!*"

But Fahd raised a hand calmly.

"*No, no, brother. It's a stingray. I won't jump.*"

He smiled.

"*Look. No horns.*"

He pointed to the creature's broad, flat head. Nuro nodded. Then, after minutes, another form rose on the radar.

Fahd lit up.

"*Come, baby. Come!*"

A Manta ray. Wingspan over 20 feet. As its mouth opened and its cephalic horns stretched wide to feed, Fahd tossed his lassos forward. Both horns inside the loops. Perfect catch. Then he jumped back into the water. A few seconds later, Fahd appeared at the surface, riding his Manta.

But he was shaky, his body tense, unbalanced.

From the Gerridion, Chad shouted:

"*Relax,* Fahd*!*

Let your body sleep, stretch, breathe, and calm yourself!"

Fahd tried. He managed to guide his Manta, barely. But he couldn't bank anymore. Eventually, he released himself about a mile from the Gerridion and returned slowly.

As he climbed aboard, Chad greeted him:

> *"Don't tense your body like that.*
>
> *A small tilt is enough to steer the ray."*
>
> *"Stretch your legs to slow down.*
>
> *Pull them in to speed up."*

Nuro stepped forward. Finally, the moment had come to tell his brothers about his decision. He was ready to speak.

> *"Brothers... I wanted to tell you something.*
>
> *The thing I meant to say before.*
>
> *I want to bring things back, like they were before..."*

But Chad wasn't listening. He was muttering to himself again.

"Chad," Nuro called, louder now. *"It's important. Please, listen to me."*

But Chad cut him off.

> *"No, no, no, no.*
>
> *No tricks, my brother."*

He grinned.

> *"It's your turn now.*

After you ride the ray, you can say whatever you want.

But for now, no excuses."

Nuro hesitated. Then gave a slight nod. "*All right.*" He removed his medical belt.

Chad stepped in, checking the equipment.

"*If you don't manage the ray,*" he said,

"*Just hit this red button to eject.*"

Nuro nodded until he noticed Chad reaching for a small can of krill with no label.

"*What's that?*" Nuro asked.

"*Krill,*" Chad said quickly.

"*They're laced with low levels of Gravitron.*

For you, for a smoother flight."

Chad smiled too quickly. Spoke too fast.

"*You just need to relax. Calm. Most important,*

remember,

brothers in blood and soul."

That last sentence didn't sit right. Nuro felt it. Heavy. Off. He said nothing.

Chad turned to the radar. "*There. One's approaching.*"

A Manta ray, small but fast.

"*That one's good for you,* Nuro," Chad said.

"*Are you sure?*" Nuro asked.

"*It looks big... no horns.*

"*Mantas are usually the largest. They do have hidden horns — cephalic horns. They stretch them out when they feed. So, wait for that moment, then throw the loops.*" Chad explained.

Nuro stepped to the edge of the Gerridion. The Manta swam in smooth arcs. Then, its horns stretched. Mouth open. Nuro tossed the lassos. They landed, off center.

Chad called:

"*Pull them toward you. The loop's not in the center.*"

The Manta approached the bait, still feeding. Then, at the last second, it dove deep.

Too deep. Nuro missed.

He sighed. "*Should we throw more krill?*" he asked.

"*No, no. Wait,*" Chad said.

Nuro looked at him, just for a second. In that blink, the same Manta shot up from the deep, like a bullet, straight through the loops. Nuro was stunned. He forgot to pull the lasso. He didn't even move.

Then, in one violent motion, he was uprooted from the Gerridion. Pulled off the deck, dragged into the ocean.

Down. Gone.

Vanished into the deep before his brothers could react. Even Kato was stunned. Fahd and Kato rushed to the edge of the boat. They looked right. Then left. Then right again.

Waiting. Scanning. Expecting him to surface. But there was nothing. Meanwhile, Chad sat quietly. He wrapped his arms around himself, each hand clenching the opposite arm.

Silent.

On Orun's land, the Amazigh leader—Taziri's father—entered her room. She was alone. Quiet. Her face was heavy with worry. He knew that look well. *"What's wrong, girl?"* he asked softly.

Taziri stood. She walked to him, kissed his hand, and hugged him tightly.

"I don't know," she whispered.

"I'm just... worried."

He smiled gently. *"Yes. I know that. But why?"*

She stayed silent.

He waited. Then he said quietly: *"Nuro?"*

She said nothing.

He nodded. *"He was here yesterday. He spoke to me."*

Taziri looked up, surprised.

"Father...You didn't tell me."

He smiled.

"Why should I tell you?

You act like you didn't know.

But you did know, girl."

"Father…"

"You want to know what he wanted?"

She nodded.

"He proposed."

Taziri's face lit up, slowly. She listened, quietly smiling. Then she asked: *"What did you tell him?"*

He looked at her with soft, teasing eyes.

"I told him…

If my girl agrees, then I will agree."

She broke into a smile.

"Of course I agree, Father.

Did you tell him that?"

He raised a brow.

"Matters like this don't move so quickly, girl.

Patience is an art."

She groaned, laughing.

"Father…That's not one of my talents…Waiting."

He chuckled. *"I know."* Then he grew a little more serious.

"*But tell me, girl, why are you so worried about him?*"

Taziri hesitated.

"*I don't know.*

I just…

I have this strange feeling.

Like something isn't right.

There's no reason. It just came. Now."

He looked at her carefully. Then nodded.

"*Then go…Go see him.*"

"*I can't,*" she said. "*He's at ocean. With his brothers.*"

"*Then wait,* Taziri,*" he said kindly.

She looked at him, then rolled her eyes with a smile.

"*Wait,*" she repeated softly. "*Not again.*"

In a second, Nuro was pulled into the water. He didn't even get the chance to breathe. The Manta dove straight down, fast and rageous. Like a tuna fish. Nuro's adrenaline surged, ringing in his ears. He started counting:... Six. Seven. Eight. Ten.

The Manta should head back up any moment now. They usually surface seconds after feeding on the krill with the Gravitron, which causes them to float almost immediately.

But it didn't. It kept going.

Deeper.

Nuro tried to pull the lasso gently to steer the ray. But she kept descending.

He pulled harder, right, then left, still nothing. No response.

The Manta was wild, unstoppable, or worse, as if being pulled down by something unseen.

The oxygen in Nuro's body ran low. His chest contracted, sucking inward violently against his sealed mouth, hiccup-like spasms shaking his ribs.

He slammed his thumb against the red ejection button.

Nothing.

He pressed again.

Again.

Still nothing.

The arm braces were locked to his arms like handcuffs, tight, sealed.

He began to panic. He violently pulled the lasso and kicked the ray, hoping to get its attention. He hit it and kicked again.

Let me go!

Still, nothing.

They kept descending. And then, Nuro felt something strange, a flicker of familiarity.

Déjà vu?. I've seen this... before. The sight around him. The pressure. The silence.

And then the fire began. Lava inside his chest. His lungs burned, like a trapped, starving wild animal scratching to escape. His chest buckled. His diaphragm jerked. Every part of him begged for air.

But none came.

Salty water entered his ears. His skull rang with pain. The world turned brown. Brown everywhere.

The salty water rushed into his nose.

At the end, his mouth opened.

And the beast in his chest was freed. But it inhaled only seawater.

Nuro screamed, underwater.

The sound drowned in the ocean. His tears dissolved into the salty water.

His limbs convulsed, arms, legs, chest twisting.

Then, Stillness.

No more pain.

No more lava.

No more sound.

His heart stopped pounding.

His lungs stopped fighting.

His eyes closed.

And everything turned dark.

On the surface of the ocean, Fahd and Kato scanned the surface, waiting for Nuro to reappear. But he didn't. Fahd ran to the stern of the Gerridion, hoping to see a surfacing ripple. Nothing.

Chad sat calmly, hiding the unmarked krill canister behind his back.

Fahd turned, alarmed: "Chad, *we're past ten seconds. Where is Nuro?*"

Chad replied smoothly:

> *"Count again. No panic.*
>
> *Mantas are slow risers.*
>
> *I'll count this time."*

But Fahd didn't wait. He dove into the water. Moments later, Chad followed, but not before dropping the unmarked can into the ocean.

Underwater, Chad laughed. He danced. He moved as if he were at his wedding.

Then he surfaced—his face twisted.

Screaming.

His voice cracking, desperate:

> "Kato*!*
>
> *Make a rescue call!*
>
> *We need dragons, **NOW! NOW**"*

Not far off, Fahd was also shouting: *"Nuro! Nuro!"* He swam hard to the other side of the Gerridion, calling his brother's name again and again.

Kato remained on deck.

"I called them. Dragons will arrive in minutes."

Twelve dragons arrived soon after. Their leader climbed onto the Gerridion.

"What happened?"

Chad explained every detail, calm, calculated.

"When was the last time you saw him?" the leader asked.

"About thirty minutes ago."

The leader nodded, then gave orders: two search teams:

One to scan the ocean floor.

Another to sweep the surface by air.

As they worked, Chad noticed Kato pouring something into the water.

"What are you doing?" Chad asked.

"Fish oil" Kato said flatly.

Chad shook his head.

"You don't need that."

"At least I'm doing something," Kato snapped.

"This might attract his ray."

Chad waved him off.

"The dragons are here. Let them do it."

But Kato kept pouring.

Fahd swam for over an hour. Exhausted, he finally climbed back aboard the Gerridion. He checked the echo radar screen. Nothing. No rays. No Nuro.

He is gone.

Four hours had passed since the last contact with Nuro. The twin sun had begun to sink. Darkness crept in. The leader of the rescue mission turned to the sons of Okasha.

"Majesty," he said, *"how was our Crown Prince before he began to ray?"*

Chad answered quietly, *"He was just... normal. But he insisted on removing his medical belt, even though it was important for him. I told him not to. I begged him. But he insisted."*

The rescue leader nodded grimly, then asked to search Nuro's personal belongings.

Inside, they found a canister of Gravitron antidote.

Chad and Fahd froze. Speechless. Staring at the small container as if it were a bomb.

Then Chad shouted, his voice cracking,

"Our Crown Prince would never hurt himself. Never!"

The leader answered calmly,

"Majesty, we will continue searching until we find him. But it is cold now. Dark. Perhaps you should return to the harbor."

In Orun, rumors spread like a virus, silent, invisible, and unstoppable:

The Crown Prince had taken the Gravitron antidote.
He had let himself sink into the deep ocean.
He had... taken his own life.

Taziri had been right. Her worrying was not in vain. She had felt something, pure and true. When she heard the rumors, she ran. She ran straight to the harbor.

Night had already fallen over the water at the harbor. Okasha, Taziri's father, stood waiting on the pier with others. Silent. Watching, waiting for Okasha's sons to return. The silence was shattered by the sound of Taziri's shallow, rapid breaths. Her heart pounded so fiercely.

Then the Gerridion arrived. The three sons stepped down onto the pier. Okasha said nothing. Showed nothing. As if he had already prepared for this loss. The loss of Nuro—the fourth pearl—just as it had been written and seen in his Unabii.

Chad was crying. He held Nuro's medical belt in his hand. In a broken voice, he said, *"Manta took our brother to the bottom of the ocean. We lost him."*

Fahd stared at the ground. Still. Speechless.

Then Chad turned. He met Taziri's eyes from across the pier. Then, he looked down. At her body. A look she would never forget.

She screamed, *"He's not dead! You madman!"* She tore the medical belt from Chad's hand, mounted her horse, and vanished into the night.

She rode toward the shore through the darkness until she was gone from their sight.

Something inside her still believes.

She knew it.

He was still alive. She believed it.

She is a believer.

In the ocean's deep water, Nuro's body floated in the darkness. Still. Silent. Then—a sting.

Something slapped his face.

Another. And another. Until the slaps turned sharp, biting across his cheek like a whip.

He gasped. Coughed. Vomited up saltwater.

He was alive.

When he opened his eyes, the world around him glowed faintly with an ethereal, shifting light—darkness dressed in illusion. It felt like a hallucination.

He touched his arms. The brace was still there, but no longer attached to the wild Manta. He touched his face, his skin, his chest. He could breathe. Somehow, his head was above water. The rest of his body was submerged, his back leaning against a wall beneath the surface.

He looked around, desperate for light. For a way out. There was nothing. Only thick darkness. But he didn't move, not yet. For now, the simple act of breathing felt like a miracle.

Just one breath…One breath was priceless. A gift. Even if he were to remain in this abyss forever.

It was so dark, a shark could have passed inches from his face—a hundred times—and he wouldn't have seen it.

Nuro stayed there, pressed against the wall, organizing his thoughts. Something about this place felt familiar. Again, the déjà vu. He tried to remember. He remembered the Manta pulling him down into the deep. Then, nothing.

Where am I now?

How did I end up inside this… this place?

The air was thick, stale, and damp. He touched the wall behind him, slippery and rough. It wasn't metal. Not a ship. It felt like cement.

After taking enough breath, he swam deeper into the water, searching for an exit. He reached forward, blindly feeling the walls and the floor. Nothing recognizable. Just more water. More colder. No Exit.

Then, he raised his head again, searching for the surface, but there was no surface.

Just more wall. More water.

He had drifted too far.

He was trapped.

Panic set in.

He kicked wildly, searching for the pocket of air where he could breathe. But the darkness was endless. He swam in circles, lost in his own orbit.

Then, his hand brushed something. Cables. He grabbed them. Pulled. Followed. They led him somewhere, but he wasn't sure where, so he clung to them like lifelines. Eventually, he found the surface again. Gasped.

Air.

He returned to that pocket of space, where his back met the wall, and air still awaited him.

Then again, he dived, but this time, following the cables. Returning for air. Over and over, until exhaustion weighed down his limbs like anchors.

He climbed the cables slightly, positioning his chest above the water to keep warm. He sat there in silence. But the silence didn't last.

Tiny fish began nibbling at the swollen skin of his leg. He kicked them away with both feet.

Then leaned his head against the cement wall and pressed his ear against it.

He heard something—movement—faint, distant—just the fluttering of fish in deep water.

He turned back, thinking of his next step. But the air felt heavier now. It pressed into his lungs, thick and wet, forcing him to think quickly. He wiped his face, trying to stay calm. His body shivered. Then, his thoughts drifted, not to survival, but to the one he loved.

Taziri.

Not a memory. Not a thought. She was simply there, inside him, alive in his chest. Also, Amara, his mother, he wasn't longing for her. She is always with him. Beside him. She never left.

Then, through the silence, Nuro spoke:

"Hello...?

Hello...? Is anyone there?"

His voice didn't echo. It hung in the stale air, stuck, unmoving. It was as if even sound had no escape here. He paused. Then raised his voice again:

"Creator.

Oh Creator, can you hear me?"

He trembled. His voice broke.

"Please. I have only one wish.

If you hear me... just one thing.

Take care of Taziri.

Protect her.

That's all I ask."

His voice cracked again.

"I don't care if I die here. You choose. Life or death.

But if I live...

I swear, I'll go to the Barzakh.

I'll save the people of Barzakh.

I'll never return to Orun again."

He took a breath, weak and desperate.

"I regret everything that happened to the Crossers.

I didn't ask for this position.

The Crown Prince chose me; I didn't seek it."

Tears streamed down his cheeks.

"Please… Creator… don't forget her."

Then, he wept. Loud, aching sobs that echoed inside his chest. Until, slowly, the tears stopped. And a strange calm settled in.

Time disappeared. Nuro couldn't tell how long he'd been here. Even his memory of calling the Creator felt... distant.

Had I done that minutes ago? Or days?

He tugged at the hair beneath his jaw, just below the beard line. He always shaved it clean, but now, it had grown. It was rough. It felt like two days of beard had passed. Nuro remembered shaving it just before the sailing trip with his brothers. Something in him stirred.

He began pounding on the cement wall. Again. And again. Until his arms ached and his hands were raw.

Then he dunked his head underwater to cool himself. Resurfaced. Stared blankly.

And then, from nowhere, a melody itched at the back of his mind.

Soft. Faint.

He whispered it to himself in a broken voice:

"In the land of lords, la-la-la,

In the Land of lions, da-da-da,

O light upon light—O Orun, shine bright!

O Orun, lit, la-la-lit,

Lune guided us through the night.

In the heart of dreams, la-la-la,

Under skies so wide, da-da-da,

With the stars above, we find our love,

In Orun, *we reside, la-la-la"*

He repeated it. Again. And again.

Until, finally, he leaned his head against the wall and fell asleep.

The search for Nuro continued for three days. At the spot where he vanished, the dragons scanned, dived, and swept the ocean. But there was no sign of him. No body. No trace.

Even the rays that had been mapped near the ocean floor had disappeared, gone without explanation.

Every day, Kato came to the harbor. He stood at the edge, waiting, hoping that, soon, his brother's body would float to the surface. But only one person never left.

Taziri.

She stayed at the harbor day and night. She slept on the pier; her eyes fixed on the waves.

Around her waist—Nuro's medical belt.

She spoke to no one. Only to the ocean. Whispering her pain into its silence.

Sometimes, Kato saw her speaking as if Nuro were standing right in front of her in the ocean. He watched her from behind, her shoulders trembling, her lips moving.

She did this every day. She didn't lose hope.

After three days, Chad ordered the search to end.

"There's nothing left of his body," he said coldly.

"The fish got to him. There's no point continuing."

The others, friends, brothers, and searchers, left the harbor one by one and returned to Orun.

Only Taziri stayed.

Alone. With her horse.

Chad, satisfied, lingered one last time at the harbor. But he didn't leave immediately. He slipped away to a quiet, hidden place just beyond the docks. He went there to speak with the voice. The one he had begun to miss.

The voice came.

"Son," it whispered.

"I have a gift for you."

Chad smiled.

"A gift more precious than Orun *itself,"* the voice said.

"These days belong to you now.

It is your honeymoon, and you… are the groom."

Chad blinked. *"Groom?"*

"Yes," the voice answered.

*"The moon girl—*Taziri—*is your bride."*

"I know you've always watched her.

Always longed for her.

I know everything what has happened and what will come."

"She is yours.

Go…

Ask her father for her hand.

Claim her."

Chad smiled.

"Will I marry her?" he whispered.

"You will…. son.."

After Nuro fell into a deep sleep, the Unabii returned. It was the same one he had seen since birth, but this time, it was clearer. More vivid. In motion. Inside the Unabii, he began to understand. He could finally read the encrypted fate.

The bird pulling him into the sky, it wasn't a bird.

It was the wild Manta.

And it wasn't pulling him up.

It was dragging him down, into the deep ocean.

Toward the mountain.

The upside-down mountain.

The cave.

Nuro was drifting inside it now.

Asking, *what is this place?*

Until he fell.

Fell from the mountain into the cloud and was caught by the sad man.

He woke. Eyes wide.

"It's a cave! It's a cave" he gasped.

"I'm in a cave.

That's what I saw.

I will be saved."

He sat still, breathing.

"But how?

How do I escape this darkness?"

For the first time in days, Nuro believed he could be saved. He had a chance. But the question still hovered, which direction? He had tried before. Dove into the dark. Got lost, got exhausted. But now he remembered the cables. They had helped him.

He chose the right side. He would follow the cables. He would dive again.

He prepared himself—hyperventilated, filled his lungs. Took a deep breath. But then he paused. Her words returned, soft and bright in his memory:

"If I ever can't hug you—for any reason—I'll knock on this tree."

Nuro tapped the wall gently with his index finger. A quiet smile touched his lips. Then he dove.

His hands grasped the cables beneath the water, pulling hard. Stroke by stroke, he glided forward.

But nothing came.

No light.

No sound.

Just cold.

His lungs began to beg. His chest jerked. He feared that even if he reached the surface, there might be no air. No space. Just water and wall. But he pushed upward. And finally, broke through.

There was air. Old and heavy, but enough.

He gasped. Rested. Held the cables. Then climbed slightly, positioning his chest above the water for warmth.

"*Hello*?" he called.

"*Hello? Is anyone there?*"

No echo. Just stillness.

He explored the space with his arms—Another air pocket—almost the same size as the last.

Fear struck him.

Have I gone in a circle?

Am I trapped in a maze?

Still, he dove again. Pulled the cables, moved forward. This time, not far below, his head hit something, a wall. And the cables ended.

He reached forward, feeling blindly, a wheel. Slimy. Slippery.

He gripped it and turned. It was attached to a gate. He turned again. And again. The gate opened.

A surge of water pushed him backward, pressure exploding from behind it.

Then light.

Faint, blue, blurred.

He swam forward through the gate. Toward the source of light. Through a large opening in the ceiling of the wall. He broke through it. He was outside.

Free.

In the deep, open ocean.

He turned back—One last look.

There it was:

Not a cave.

Not a mountain.

But the abandoned hyperloop. His prison. The wild, intelligent Manta had brought him there, not to drown him, but to save his life.

He looked up. There it was: The surface. Far above, but real.

He swam. And swam.

And then—time stopped.

The water thickened. His motion slowed. It felt like he had been swimming for hours.

Weeks.

Maybe since his birth.

He was suspended—not moving.

Not sinking.

Just… existing.

Who am I?

Where did I come from?

What am I doing here?

His mind was empty—a blue, featureless memory.

But one instinct remained:

Swim.

He kicked. He fought.

He reached the surface.

Light.

Sunlight.

Air.

He gasped. His vision was blurred. His eyes could barely open.

And then, he smelled it.

Offensive. *That smell...of Death.*

He coughed and called out:

> *"Help!* Kato! Chad! Fahd!
>
> *I'm here!*
>
> *I'm alive!"*

No answer. Just water. Blue, endless blue.

He turned slowly. Behind him stood the Panthalassic wall. He was on the other side.

Barzakh!

Panic rose.

> *No one can reach me here.*
>
> *No one even knows I'm alive.*

He turned again. Scanned the surface. Then, he saw something floating nearby. Orange.

He swam toward it with what little strength he had left. Grabbed it with both arms and laid his head on it.

A life jacket.

He didn't have the strength to wear it. He just clung to it, breathing. Surviving. He gathered his breath, tried to hold onto his energy, but it didn't last long. Something brushed his leg. He kicked reflexively. Then he forced himself upright and slid the lifejacket on. He looked down, a large fish passed by and swam away. Fear surged through him. He almost swam away too… but then, ahead, he saw another lifejacket.

And beyond that…

Thousands.

Waves rolled and revealed them, a floating field of lifejackets.

He swam forward.

And then he saw—not life…

But death.

He screamed:

"No!

No, no, no!"

He wept.

"No…"

All around him were the Crossers.

Not just gone.

Torn apart.

Shark-bitten.

Half-eaten.

Legs here. Arms there.

Empty vests over water.

He swam between them, searching, *"Anyone!?"*

But there was no one. Only silence.

Then, he looked at his own hands.

Paused. Stared.

The same scars.

The same nails.

But the skin—white.

White as milk.

He looked at his arms.

His chest.

Snow white.

Then Professor Casablanca stopped. He walked to his suitcase and pulled out a sealed-up clear glass bottle of water.

He held it upright. Then turned it sideways. Then upside down.

I asked:

"What happened?

How did Nuro *survive underwater?"*

He held the bottle out and smiled.

"See this?" he said.

"That air bubble inside? That's an air pocket."

"It's filled with oxygen.

Limited, but enough."

"If I threw this sealed bottle into the ocean, it would sink.

But the air bubble would remain—trapped.

As long as the seal is good, the air can last."

"These air pockets aren't magic.

They're real.

Found in many sunken ships."

"And that old air,

even stale,

is priceless."

He paused. Then continued:

"Nuro *was trapped inside an air pocket like this.*

Inside the abandoned hyperloop, beneath the Panthalassic wall."

"*And it wasn't a coincidence.*

The Manta brought him there."

"Rays," he added, "*are among the most intelligent sea creatures I've ever known.*"

I asked him again:

"*But what about his skin?*

And his sense of time as he was surfacing?"

Professor Casablanca nodded.

"*That was the bends.*

Also called decompression sickness."

"Nuro *had been deep in the ocean.*

When he rose vertically to the surface, the nitrogen levels in his blood spiked."

"*This is a known risk for divers,*

especially those who ascend too quickly from deep water."

"*The result? Pain. Hallucinations. Memory loss.*

Even time distortion."

"*That's why, for him, what took 30 seconds…*

felt like years.

Like he had been swimming since birth."

"But the skin?" I pressed.

"That wasn't a hallucination?"

"No," he said.

"That was real."

"It was his medical belt."

I frowned. "How?"

He explained:

"Nuro *had total albinism—a genetic condition from birth.*

A deficiency in melanin cells, the ones responsible for our skin color."

"He wore the medical belt because he was undergoing gene therapy to correct it."

"But after removing the belt and spending three days lost in the ocean,

The treatment stopped.

His skin reverted.

It lost its pigment."

"It turned white.

White like snow."

"It wasn't an Illusion.

That was his real skin."

"And yes," he added with a quiet smile,

"He was born blue, because of asphyxia.

*The umbilical cord was wrapped around his neck.
Remember?"*

Then Professor Casablanca continued:

"After escaping, Nuro *drifted. He gathered the life jackets around him and made a raft out of them. And laid his body over it."*

"Just like the cloud in his Unabii."

"But dehydration set in.

Thirst began to beat him."

"Cracks appeared on his lips. His vision blurred.

And again, he saw only pictures."

"A hand. Reaching down from a boat.

Pulling him up."

"Helping him."

As it always was, a hand.

A hand that once pulled Nuro *down from the womb of his mother,* Amara.

A hand that now lifted him up from the depths of the salty ocean.

About the Author

Khaled El Hendawy is an Egyptian-German vascular surgeon whose debut novel, *Heaven of Orun*, began not as a manuscript—but as a vision. The story first came to him in dreams in 2009, then followed him into waking life until he could no longer ignore it. What started as a haunting glimpse of another world became the first part of a powerful trilogy.

This book is his answer.

Part 2 will be released on September 5th, 2026.

To follow quotes and moments from *Heaven of Orun*, scan the code and connect on Instagram.

@KHALED_EL_HENDAWY

Cover design by: Menna Shaqran (Menna3850@gmail.com), Instagram menna_shaqran.

Interior design and formatting by: Khaled El Hendawy

ISBN: 979-8-9993067-0-8

For permissions, rights, or inquiries, contact:

Khaled.e@mail.de

www.ingramcontent.com/pod-product-compliance
Lightning Source LLC
Chambersburg PA
CBHW052041240626
47153CB00006B/2188